187902

GW00598849

Goodbye, Pussy

She was dazed and wandering when the police found her, apparently suffering from severe nervous strain. It was late, she was alone, and her car had just gone out of control and grazed a lamp-post near her home in London. Could that alone have brought her to such a pass?

The woman in question was beautiful Kate Hawksmoor, brilliant painter, semi-recluse, and widow of a wealthy businessman who had died mysteriously when his car went over a cliff in Cornwall shortly before their only child was born. Now three-year-old Pussy was missing, and far from being frantic, Kate had not reported it, was determinedly blocking all enquiries, and was even prepared to lie about the child's whereabouts. When the police learned that she had recently made a distressing discovery about her husband, their fears for Pussy and their suspicion of Kate grew.

Bit by bit the case against her built up to a frightening accusation. Then she gave the police the slip ... Not until the last pages of this unusual and gripping murder story is the truth about Pussy revealed.

SARAH KEMP

Goodbye, Pussy

COLLINS, ST JAMES'S PLACE, LONDON

William Collins Sons & Co. Ltd
London · Glasgow · Sydney · Auckland
Toronto · Johannesburg

First published 1979
© Sarah Kemp 1979
ISBN 0 00 231268 9
Set in Baskerville
Made and Printed in Great Britain by
William Collins Sons & Co. Ltd, Glasgow

To C.D.P.R. and S.G.M for
their unstinted help always

CHAPTER I

THE PROBING FINGERS of the car headlights picked out a
signpost by the side of the rutted lane ahead: *Trewinn
Farm – Camping*, then moved across a sea of wet gorse,
sheeting rain, dead heads of poppies – as a spin of the
steering-wheel sent the big vehicle lumbering over
slippery, sheep-nibbled turf. Too fast: the driver had to
stab hard upon the brake when the cliff edge came up
unexpectedly soon.

Beyond and below was a waste of water; white
breakers clawing at the base of the granite wall, fangs
of rock close offshore. The edge of the land, in a desola-
tion of darkness and rain.

The driver was ill-clad for the enterprise, and got
soaked through in the struggle to heft a heavy suitcase
from out of the car's capacious boot and drag the
cumbersome burden through the muddy grass to the
cliff edge.

A pause for breath; a chance to look down into the
seething maelstrom below; to see it as some hellish pit
of wild beasts, baying and scrabbling for meat to be
thrown down . . .

A final effort. A tip of the suitcase, a push with a
foot – and it was gone; spinning over and over;
momentarily lost from sight, then sharply silhouet-
ted against a sudden blossoming of white water. It

struck well clear of the base of the cliff and sank immediately.

'Goodbye!' breathed the figure on the high edge. 'Goodbye, Pussy!'

CHAPTER II

SUMMONED BY a telephone call from the police, Colin and Cynthia Brierley came to Kate Hawksmoor's studio flat off The Boltons and were admitted by a uniformed woman sergeant.

'It's Mr Brierley. This is my wife.'

'Come in, please, sir. The doctor's with Mrs Hawksmoor right now.'

'Is she – ? I mean, what happened? "Found wandering"? It seems – I mean – such a funny thing to be found doing.' Cynthia Brierley had a pretty, vapid face, with a *retroussé* nose that wrinkled during the expressing of distaste. Like her husband, she was dressed in 'good' tweeds, country brogues. The police sergeant, who was young and discerning, cast them as suburbanites of the golf-club and saloon bar sort.

'There's not a lot I can tell you, ma'am,' replied the sergeant. 'A constable on duty in the King's Road found Mrs Hawksmoor wandering in a dazed and distressed manner in the early hours of this morning and took her to the station. She was unable to give an account of herself, you see, but was identified from the contents of her handbag. By the same means, they were able to establish that she was the owner of a Rolls-Royce that had been found crashed against a lamp-post and abandoned just off Hammersmith Road an hour or so earlier.'

'We saw the Rolls out in the drive,' said Brierley. 'Fine state it's in. All covered in mud and with the radiator bashed in.' He sounded affronted.

'What about the child?' demanded Cynthia Brierley. 'Where's little Priscilla?'

'Child, ma'am?' The sergeant looked puzzled and shook her head. 'I've had no information about any child.'

'Her child,' said Brierley. 'My cousin's child.'

'That's her – over there,' said his wife, pointing.

They were in a large, airy, split-level studio room, decorated with dark blue seating units, a few excellent Persian rugs, a vast and unexpected *armoire* in rosewood flanked by tubular steel chairs. The far end was a litter of artist's gear: a table smothered in paint-streaked tubes, vases stuffed with brushes, a palette. Set upon an antique easel was a canvas bearing a life-sized, full-length portrait of a child of about three, with wistful eyes, blonde plaits, and carrying a teddy-bear. The figure was finished, but the background had been only lightly sketched in with thin paint.

'That's her, right enough,' said Brierley. 'Damned good likeness, too. Not that I'm any judge of art.'

'Bit of a change from her usual style,' said Cynthia Brierley. 'All those dirty nudes.' She wrinkled her nose in distaste.

The sergeant said: 'Well, the child isn't in the flat, so she's probably in someone's care. Mrs Hawksmoor will be able to enlighten you as soon as the doctor says you may see her. She's a widow, isn't she?'

'Three years,' said Cynthia Brierley. 'He was Giles

Hawksmoor, you know. Very big in the City. Left her half a million, not counting property. He died very tragically. Mr Brierley was his only blood relation. I suppose Kate must have had some sort of nervous breakdown, is that it?'

'I don't know, ma'am,' said the sergeant. 'The doctor will be able to tell you that.'

' 'Sfunny, isn't it, darling?' demanded Cynthia Brierley. 'Kate having such a thing as a nervous breakdown, I mean. So cold and unemotional, I've always thought her.'

'Quite, darling,' confirmed Brierley. 'Very chill and withdrawn sort of person is Kate. But very artistic – and there's hidden depths in the artistic kind. Sort of, you know, unpredictable.'

There was a tread on stairs beyond an archway at the far end of the studio. 'Here comes the doctor now,' said the sergeant.

The physician was youngish, big, imperturbable-looking. As he entered the studio room, he glanced at the watch on his thick wrist and checked it with a long-case clock in the corner.

'Ah, Doctor, I'm Mr Brierley, cousin to Mrs Hawksmoor's late husband. How's the patient?'

The other took Brierley's proffered hand. 'She's calmer now,' he said. 'I've sedated her slightly. You can go up and see her, but don't stay long. She should sleep. I'll call around tomorrow and see how she is. Is there any help in the house?'

'She won't have any help,' said Cynthia Brierley. 'Does everything for herself. She's very independent.

Very – *capable*.' She made it sound like a dirty word.

'Well, I would advise some help,' said the doctor. 'For a week or so, at least.'

'And to look after the child,' said Cynthia Brierley.

The physician glanced at her, puzzled. 'There's a child?' he asked. 'I had no idea. Mrs Hawksmoor never mentioned a child. I clearly had the impression from her that she was alone in the place.'

'Dr Manners isn't Mrs Hawksmoor's regular doctor,' explained the sergeant. 'We called him in. Mrs Hawksmoor wasn't in any condition to give the name of her regular man.'

'Well, I'm worried about that child,' said Cynthia Brierley, 'I really am. I shan't rest till I know the little mite's safe and well and in good hands. Come on, Colin. Let's go and see her.'

'I'll not go till you come down again, Mr Brierley,' said the sergeant. 'Just in case there's any – misunderstanding – concerning the whereabouts of the child. What did you say her name was?'

'Priscilla,' replied Brierley.

'*She* insists on calling her "Pussy",' said his wife. 'Did you ever hear such a name to give a kiddie?'

The stuff that the strange doctor had given Kate Hawksmoor had the effect of making everything seem further away; of distancing thought, sense of touch, even the small sounds that came in through the open window of her bedroom: a car changing gear round the corner, birds in the trees, a far-off lawn-mower. She closed her eyes and let herself drift with the tide of forgetting; opened them at the sound of a tap upon her door.

'It's Cynth and Colin. May we come in, dear?'

Kate experienced a momentary panic, which showed that the stuff the doctor had given her was by no means an impregnable barrier against the outer world.

'Hello,' she heard herself whisper. 'Yes, please do come in.'

She did not like her cousins-in-law, but it had nothing to do with their careful accents, their snobbishness, the appalling roundelay of middle-class pretentiousness; the Acacia Avenue gentility that Giles had found so contemptible, so risible; that he had been able to mimic and extemporize upon so brilliantly, so cruelly. She simply did not like them as fellow human beings. Cynthia struck her as being heartless; Colin – it really was absurd – as a criminally-inclined person.

'Dear old Kate. What have you been up to, silly girl?' Cynthia had plumped herself down upon the edge of her bed and was treating her to a false smile of comradeship. 'Wandering about on your own at all hours of the night, not to mention smashing up that lovely Rolls. And where's Priscilla?'

Kate felt her mouth go suddenly dry.

'Pussy . . .' she whispered.

Cynthia shrugged and wrinkled up her nose. 'If you like,' she said huffily. 'Where's Pussy?'

'She – she's away.'

'Well, that's a relief at any rate,' said Cynthia. 'Who's she staying with?'

'With . . .'

'Yes?'

'With Nannie.'

'Oh, that old thing. Is she still alive? Surely she's not still capable of looking after a three-year-old. Look – what do you say to Colin and me fetching her back to our place for a week or so till you're back on your feet again?'

'No . . .' She heard her own voice waver with panic.

'As you like,' said Cynthia, affronted. 'But it really would be no trouble at all. We've got a swimming pool in the patio now, did you know? Kidney-shaped. And she could come to the Country Club with us on Sunday afternoon. We'll give her the time of her life and you'll be free of worries just when you shouldn't be worrying, you really shouldn't. Aren't I right, Colin darling?'

'Right as ever, darling,' responded her husband, stroking the silky, military-style moustache that was a relic of his army days. By Jove, he thought, eyeing his cousin-in-law, she's not what you'd call an obvious beauty. But those big brown go-to-bed eyes, not to mention what one can see of her figure under that nightie . . . Steady, Brierley!

'Then it's settled,' said Cynthia. 'We'll drive to fetch her tomorrow, first thing. Where does Nannie live now – is it far?'

If only she could think quicker; anticipate the pitfalls ahead before they yawned beneath her feet; but the stuff the doctor had given her was having an ever more marked effect. Cynthia and Colin were become like distant silhouettes performing behind a sheet, their shapes thrown upon it by a flickering candle.

'I – I've forgotten,' she whispered.

'Forgotten?' Cynthia eyed her with total contempt mingled with flat disbelief. 'How can you possibly have forgotten? Is it in London? Or in the country?'

'In – in the country.'

'Where in the country?'

'Goudley.'

Brierley exclaimed: 'Ah, Goudley! You mean the cottage that Giles's people had for a weekend place. So that's where old Nannie Porter's ended up, eh? By jove, I remember her well. The old trout was ancient when she first wheeled out Cousin Giles in Kensington Gardens. Fancy her still being alive.'

'*I don't want you to take Pussy away from Goudley!*' The words exploded from Kate's lips, shocking even herself to silence.

The Brierleys looked at her, then at each other.

'Well!' said Cynthia. 'If that's how you feel about it, we might as well leave. Only trying to do our best to help. But there you are.' She sniffed, got up from the bed.

'Please – I'm sorry,' said Kate. 'It was very rude of me. But I'm . . .'

'You're not yourself today,' said Cynthia, softening, seizing upon the polite formula. 'Well, we'll leave you to get some sleep, dear. And I'll ring you tomorrow. Oh, I'd almost forgotten. You must get someone in to look after you.'

'I don't want . . .'

There was no checking the torrent of words. Thank-

fully, they were muffled by distance and by the weari-
ness of mind that now all but encompassed her. She
closed her eyes and let the droning drift around, un-
heard, inside her head. And then she slept.

Kate woke in the pinky light of sunset, roused by the
sound of the Venetian blinds flapping and clacking in
the evening breeze. She got out of bed, closed the
window and straightened the blinds.

From the bathroom, she wandered out on to the
landing, shrugging on her dressing-gown. There was
no need to switch on the staircase lights; the huge
windows of the studio admitted the sunset. She felt
curiously light-headed. There was an alien taste in her
mouth, and this prompted her to get a glass of water,
which she then took through the archway that led to
Giles's study; three steps up, and there was his desk,
his old-fashioned roll-top office desk – just as he had
left it: a jumble of papers still littering the blotter; the
red, black, and green ballpoints still in place in the
antique penholder; his brass carriage clock, still un-
wound, telling the time of one-thirty.

Memories . . .

Memories of their first meeting.

Her first, her very first Bond Street show. A 'one-
man' show, furthermore, and she but a year out of the
Royal College of Art, wearing – as she recalled it so
clearly – a cool and extremely subdued dress in Indian
silk, with only a pendant of a Roman coin for jewellery.
She had spotted him at once: tall and fair like a Viking,
a Viking incongruous in clerical, city grey, hard

collar, slender gold watch-chain swagged across an exceedingly flat tummy. It was the eyes – those questing, humorous, quizzical, shrewd eyes – that had held her. And had won her.

'I'm Giles Hawksmoor. I think your pictures are lovely. Come to that, Miss Gregg, I think that you're lovely, too.'

Pleasant, and easy to counter.

'Thank you, Mr Hawksmoor. "We aim to please." And what, pray, Mr Hawksmoor, do *you* do?'

'Madam, I am Something in the City,' was his response.

'I am vastly impressed,' was her reply. They both had laughed.

Mr Grosse, senior partner of Moorwood, Banks & Grosse, who had 'taken on' the entirely unknown Kate Gregg solely on the score of a laudatory, yet almost completely incomprehensible, notice of her pictures in a Young Contemporaries' exhibition, had been much aggrieved to observe his young protégée depart from the Private View at a very early hour in the company of that same gentleman whom, upon enquiry, the delighted gallery owner later had discovered to have purchased each and every one of Kate Gregg's exhibited pictures unsold and available.

Later, lying together, side by side, arms entwined, blandly satiated, she idly traced the small discoloration on his chest. 'What's that, Giles?'

'It's a wound.'

'Wound – what kind of wound?'

'My brother, he shot me with a shotgun.'

'You are joking! Giles, you are putting me on!'

'No. Honestly. This was at a pheasant shoot in Suffolk. My brother, he's at the far side of a hedge, I'm on the other. A pheasant takes off out of the hedge and Joe's reactions are so fast that he's got off a barrel before he realizes that I'm right in his line of fire. Here – feel.' Guided by his hand, her finger gently probed and found a tiny hardness beneath the skin that moved to her touch. 'That's a number of six shotgun pellet. The rest of 'em they got out easily. This one eventually worked its way to the surface. I could have it cut out, but I've grown quite attached to it. A *memento mori* of poor old Joe that I'll carry to my own grave, I suppose.'

'Your brother – he's dead?'

Yes, Joe was dead. Neither then, nor even after, had he shown any inclination to talk about him. There were no other relations save Colin and Cynthia Brierley to witness their wedding at Caxton Hall in the spring of that year and the Brierleys were on holiday; so there were only Giles's fellow partners from the old family firm of Lloyds brokers, a few members of the Newmarket racing set, the adjutant of his old regiment. They had been blissfully happy on that golden day, and she, Kate, had worn pale lilac . . .

She set the glass down upon the edge of a low table, fumbled, and dropped it. The broken pieces skittered across the parquet. In picking them up, she cut her finger, and the bright blood startled her. Binding a handkerchief round the wound, she quitted the room with a sudden feeling of unease.

She re-entered the studio; met her reflection in a long mirror beyond the easel. She looked drawn and pale, unhealthily greenish in the half-tones, and her straight black hair hung in rats' tails about her shoulders. Brushing the tendrils from her cheek, she was horrified to see a streak of blood from her crude bandage appear above her eye, and wiped it off hastily.

Her painting table was in a dreadful mess, but what can one expect with an inquisitive child about the place? Things had been so much easier when Nannie was here. She straightened the brushes in the pots, put the piles of tubes in some sort of order, and succeeded in getting smears of thick paint on her hands and then on to her dressing-gown. The paint rag with which she tried to remove the stains was damp with dirty paraffin and only succeeded in making matters irreparably worse. Somewhat to her surprise, she found that she was crying uncontrollably.

The crunch of footfalls on the gravel drive outside the window checked her paroxysm. They stopped. She tiptoed, barefoot, over to the window, lifted a slat of the Venetian blind and peered out and down.

A tall man in a dark suit stood with his back to her. He was examining the front of the Rolls, which was parked by a bank of laurel bushes half-way between the entrance to the drive and the door of the flat. She bit her lip, as he reached out and ran a hand over the dented radiator and the deep crease in the offside wing. The action of stooping caused him to present his profile to her. He looked to be thirty-ish, dark-haired

and dark-skinned enough to be an Arab. A considerable number of rich Arabs had taken houses in the
vicinity; Kate found them curiously disturbing,
though she had never so much as exchanged a glance
with any of them.

Having finished his inspection of the car, the stranger
turned and walked towards the door – her door. In
doing so, he appeared in full face. If an Arab, she
thought, then a blue-eyed Arab.

The doorbell rang twice. A minute later, it rang
again. She waited by the window, allowing herself
only the lightest and most silent of breaths, willing all
the time for her heart to quieten its noisy pounding.

Two steps on the gravel: she imagined him to have
moved back in order to look up at the windows. With
an intense surge of relief, she then heard him walk
swiftly away, down the drive – pausing for a moment
when he came abreast of the Rolls – and out into the
street.

Slowly, she opened her eyes.

She did not dare to switch on the lights, but sat
motionlessly in the studio, gazing at a blank wall, her
mind a slate wiped clean of all recollection, unaware of
the passing of time. The discreet pulsing of the telephone on the table beside her jolted her to a kind of
awareness. Her hand hovered for some moments over
the instrument, then returned to her lap. The ringing
persisted. As much as to silence it as for any other
reason, she picked it up.

'Yes?' she whispered.

'Excuse, please. Is this Mrs Hawksmoor speaking?'

It was a man's voice, deep in timbre and thickly accented.

With trembling hand, she fumbled the receiver back on to its cradle. Across the dark room, caught in a thin shaft of moonlight, the eyes of the child in the painting gazed unwaveringly at her. It was the only time since first entering the studio that she had brought herself to look at the portrait.

'Pussy!' whispered Kate Hawksmoor brokenly. And then; 'Pussy! Oh, why did it have to happen?'

CHAPTER III

LATE AT NIGHT, between waking and sleeping, Kate
Hawksmoor had a vision of a pictorial composition that
afforded her both a means of taking inner stock of herself and of tackling an absorbing problem in paint.
And, anyhow, she could not get to sleep.

Slipping on her painting smock, she descended to the
studio; took down from the easel the almost finished
portrait of Pussy and laid it against the wall, face out-
wards.

There was a small stack of fresh canvases, all ready-
primed and painted with the buff-coloured undercoat
upon which she preferred to work. She chose one that
was three feet by two, set it up on the easel, landscape.
Closed her eyes and looked inside her head.

The vision was of a large and dimly-lit apartment
that was circular in shape and entirely surrounded with
doors. Locked doors.

Taking up a sable-hair brush, she dipped it in
turpentine, then in paint – burnt umber. Facing the
canvas, and narrowing an eye, she drew a bold, un-
hesitating stroke across it from left to right, about a
third of the way from the bottom; a slightly curving
arc, rising in the middle. A segment of the circular
apartment, as seen from the middle of its floor. It was a
pity that one could not encompass the entire circle in
one flat plane. No matter; there were too many doors

encircling the room; the vital ones numbered no more than, say, five.

With the tip of the brush, she sketched in the shape of five tall doors along the curved line – adding part of a sixth at the right-hand edge, to provide a sense of imbalance and tension.

With the creative end of her mind coolly absorbed in the practised techniques of her art, the evasive part of her consciousness roamed freely – and largely un-controlled – over the labyrinth of her life, past, present, future. She made some attempts to direct her thoughts, and was uncomfortably aware that there were dark areas from which her mind recoiled. These, she told herself, were the locked doors.

Now she was working with two colours: a grey and a muted green; employing quite thick paint, scumbling it broadly over the width of the canvas, allowing it to be modulated, as both chance and necessity dictated, by the buff-coloured undercoat.

Next, taking a clean brush, which she loaded with a mid-blue she sketched in the outline of the first door from the left, giving the impression of daylight beyond.

She had opened the first door to her memories. It had not been so painful, after all. But, then, the memory beyond it was, though far from bland, not of the sort from which she would flinch. No unbearable pain behind this particular door. Later, when she came ot certain others, the story would be different. But now...

I remember the day that I found Giles out in a lie. It was a Thursday afternoon and I rang him at the office. Miss Gilliam, his secretary, seemed quite surprised. Mr Giles (he

*had been 'Mr Giles' ever since he joined the family business as
a junior partner straight from Cambridge) wasn't to be expected
back save for half an hour at the end of the afternoon, when
he came in to sign his letters. It was Thursday, you see.*

Oh, was it?

*With no more than an imp of curiosity, I asked him, that
evening, if he had had an interesting day. A routine day, he told
me. And why had I phoned him?*

*I knew he was lying, for he had a way of avoiding one's
eye when he dissembled – which was not often. The following
Thursday, I rang his office again, just after lunch. Giving Miss
Gilliam a trumped-up explanation of urgency, I said that,
Thursday or no Thursday, I must reach him immediately, and
did he not give her a number to phone him at in an emergency?
Yes, indeed he did. And she gave it to me.*

*That evening, puzzled, somewhat amused, and very slightly
uneasy, I tackled him over dinner:*

*'Darling, why have you been taking flying lessons on the
quiet every week?'*

*He nearly dropped his wine glass; coloured up like a little
boy who's been caught stealing jam.*

'How – how did you know that, Kate?'

*'Was it supposed to be a secret? Yes, it was obviously in-
tended to be a secret. But why, darling – why?'*

*He said: 'I – simply wanted to surprise you one day.
Drive you to the airfield, casually climb into a plane and take
off.' He grinned, and his eyes never wavered. I could have
reached across and hugged him.*

*'Darling, sometimes I think that I married a great big
schoolboy,' I told him fondly. 'But, tell me, how far have you
got with your lessons?'*

'I'm not frightfully good with my landings, but the man says he'll let me fly solo next Thursday.'

'Can I come and watch?'

'Good heavens, no.' He was quite adamant about that.

The following Wednesday evening, we went to the theatre, had a late theatre supper – and a most appalling row. I sometimes tell myself it was all my fault; but I am being more than charitable to the memory of my dead husband. It was Giles's fault. He had been tense and edgy all evening. He was rude to the waiter – which was quite out of character for him. When I mildly remonstrated with him for it, he told me to shut up. We slept apart that night, for the first time in our married life, he in the spare room, I alone in that huge bed.

He left the flat without saying goodbye; but I waved to him out of the window and shouted 'good luck with your solo'. He ignored me.

That whole day, I lived in dread of our meeting again; spent the time doing all the small, boring, undemanding jobs around the place; too disturbed in my mind to paint. The snarl of his Aston-Martin coming up the drive sent me into a tizz like a lovesick schoolgirl. He was two hours late and dinner was ruined, but what did I care?

'Darling, do we open a bottle of champagne in honour of your successful solo?' I had taken tremendous trouble with my appearance; wore a silk dress with a scandalous neckline that he much admired.

'No – we do not.'

He brushed past me, went straight into his study and slammed the door behind him. I heard the chink of glass on glass. He kept a tray of whisky in there. And I had noticed that he was already rather drunk.

At midnight, or later, I gave up trying not to get to sleep and went down to him. He was slumped across his desk, head pillowed in his arms. He looked round when I entered and rushed towards him.

'Oh, Kate – dear Kate.'

'Darling!'

I took his head and pressed his face against my bosom. It wrenched at my heart to see dried rivulets of tears upon his cheeks. And I had never known whisky to make him lachrymose; it had to be something more, something bigger.

'To hell with failing your bloody solo, darling,' I told him. 'What does it matter?'

And then I got the truth of it:

'I didn't fail. I never went near the bloody place.'

I had it, little by little; then in a torrent of self-loathing and despair: how the notion of learning to fly, begun upon an impulse, had gone bad on him almost immediately – which was why he had never mentioned it to me. He had hoped, in time, to conquer the physical terror that overcame him at the mere notion of one day being sent up into the air alone and without help. It had been an empty hope.

'This morning,' he told me, 'I went to the loo in the office and threw up with sheer fright. At lunch-time, I wandered round the City contriving what to do. I thought of phoning my instructor at the airfield to say that I had an important business engagement. Then I decided to keep my options open till the last moment, till two-thirty, when I was due on the tarmac. In case I summoned up the guts.

'The airfield's out on the Great West Road. I never got within five miles of it. On the way there, I saw a jumbo jet shaping up to land at Heathrow, and I was up there in my little

Piper Comanche with an empty seat by my side and the end of the runway coming up to meet me, my hands trembling and a hole in my guts. Poor Kate. Poor, dear, compassionate Kate – your big, golden-haired lover-boy is nothing but a chicken-livered, gutless . . .'

'*No – no, it isn't true!*' I told him. '*What you have is a simple phobia, no more related to true cowardice than being scared of heights, or being shut in, or snakes, or cats, or a hundred other things. You've got an aversion to flying aeroplanes. So – hooray for motor-cars!*'

'*Dear Kate. Darling Kate. Such a comfort,*' he whispered against my bosom. '*My beautiful, talented, artistic, wise and adorable little sweet-talking liar.*'

'*Don't you call me a liar, my good man,*' I countered lightly. '*Or I'll send for my big strong husband to punch you right in the bloody nose.*'

'*Kate, Kate – I've wanted to be so much to you. For your sake. For the way I love you, my Kate.*'

'*You have been – you are – everything to me,*' I whispered against his cheek. '*And now, for heaven's sake, what are we doing here at this time of a winter's night, with our nice warm bed waiting for us upstairs?*'

In the ecstatic hours left before dawn, I believe that we conceived my darling Priscilla, my Pussy, in love and mutual tenderness. And that I shall always believe . . .

The open door stood wide open for all to see. Framed against the blue sky beyond was a head, disproportionately large – of a man with hair of Viking's colour, and shrewd eyes that were clouded with self-loathing and despair.

*

It was past two o'clock in the morning when Kate laid
aside her brushes and threw herself down on the studio
sofa. Sleep was long in coming, and haunted with unease when it came. The dawn chorus of starlings and
blackbirds in the plane trees beyond the yew hedge
woke her. She rose and went to run herself a hot bath;
pausing on the way to glance critically at the painting
she had begun during the night.

Strange, she thought, how impersonal is the eye of
the trained artist, how absorbed with purely formal
values. The head of Giles was heart-rendingly evocative
of the occasion which had inspired it; yet her eye's only
concern was for the shape – and a very nice shape it
was, too – which lay between the noble dome of his
skull and the top edge of the open door. The thought
struck her, also, that she must address herself to the
opening of the second door. A shudder brought her nude
body out in gooseflesh. It was pleasant to step into the
bath and let the scented balm of warmth close about
her.

Yes, the painting, though fraught with risks, was her
only way to a kind of salvation; a way to find the understanding which might allay the dreadful guilt which
surrounded her. She remembered the man who had
been prowling in the drive: the blue-eyed Arab who
had almost certainly been the one to telephone soon
after. He – whoever he was – had had the power to
probe the edges of her guilt. What did he want of her?

The cosseting warmth presently having lost its
allure, Kate got out of the bath and, wrapping herself
in a towelling robe, went back into the studio. An hour

or so later, there came the sound of a car's tyres on the gravel drive outside. She felt her heartbeats quicken.

Shielded by the curtain, she peered out. A small saloon car was parked by her door. A man got out. Hatless, he showed a small tonsure at the crown of a mop of short, fair hair. Broad, rugby-player's shoulders under a grey hopsack jacket; a strong-looking hand upon the car door as he slammed it shut. He was carrying a black bag, and the silvery end of a stethoscope hung, snake-like from his pocket. She remembered – and half-recognized – the doctor they had brought to her.

The doorbell rang. She went to answer it, though with reluctance. Clutching at the neck of her robe, she met his eyes – they were grey and disconcerting – and looked down and away.

'May I come in?' His voice was deep and inflected with a touch of humour.

'Yes, of course. Please . . .'

She led him into the studio. He looked about him.

'You've been painting already this morning.'

She looked at him, puzzled.

'I can smell the fresh paint,' he explained.

'Oh,' she said.

He saw the newly-worked canvas on the easel and crossed over to it.

'Mmm. This is impressive. Might one enquire the subject?'

'It's – symbolic,' said Kate.

'Symbolic. Ah.' He nodded tolerantly.

'There – there's a lot still to be done,' she said. 'I've only done one session on it.'

He nodded again; switched his gaze from the canvas to Kate.

'Well, how are you this morning, Mrs Hawksmoor? You're a better colour, though you still look rather tired.'

'I – I didn't sleep very well,' said Kate.

'And got up early to start the painting.'

'No, I began it last – ' too late, she saw the trap she had sprung for herself – 'last night,' she finished lamely.

He frowned. 'I don't think I approve of that, Mrs Hawksmoor. Working late at night.'

'I – I couldn't sleep,' said Kate.

He reached out his hand, gently thumbed wide first one of her eyelids, then the other.

'You must sleep,' he said. 'I'll give you a capsule to take tonight. Shall we sit down?'

Kate took her place on the sofa, the disconcerting doctor sat at the other end; regarded her.

'Now,' he said. 'Tell me what happened the other night. I wasn't able to get any sense out of you when I saw you yesterday. You had an accident with your car, is that it? What kind of accident?'

'I – I think I ran into a lamp-post,' said Kate.

'Not with a great deal of force, you didn't,' he said. 'The damage to your lovely Rolls, though regrettable and a sin against *de luxe* engineering, scarcely amounts to more than a slight bump.'

'I was trying to do a turn in a narrow street,' said Kate, with a conscious effort to remember. 'Yes, that was it. I found myself in a cul-de-sac. It was rather –

alarming. Very dark. Factory buildings, all shut up and deserted. I was frightened.'

'Whatever brought you into a district like that, Mrs Hawksmoor?' he asked.

'I – I was chased there!' She clenched her small fists, closed her eyes.

'Chased – by whom?'

She took a deep, shuddering breath. 'It began on the motorway. I'm not a very good – I'm a very nervous – driver. Always keep in the slow lane and never go above fifty. The big lorries, the juggernauts, terrify me. The way they come up close behind one and pull out to overtake. That night – it seemed to me that they were deliberately trying to terrify me. Once, when I tried to overtake one of them, another came up alongside on the fast lane. We – we went for some distance, the three of us in line. The men in the juggernauts, the drivers, were making – obscene gestures – to each other about me. I – I could see their faces quite clearly in the lamplight.' She pressed her hands against her eyes.

He waited in patient silence for a full half-minute, and then he murmured gently: 'Yes. And then?'

Kate lowered her hands, opened her eyes.

'When I left the motorway,' she said, 'I was surrounded by a group of youths on motor-cycles. They were covered all over with badges and studs.'

'Hell's Angels,' he supplied. 'And they buzzed you – is that it?'

'Is that what they call it? Yes, they did that. Cut in very close, so that I had to brake and swerve all over the place. One of them came so close that he was able to kick the side of the car as he went past. I panicked then: went down the next turning, quite certain that they would follow me, and going faster than I have ever driven in my life before. I went – a long way. Turning here and there. In the end, I found myself up against this high wall with spikes on top. I felt trapped. I seemed to hear the roar of their motor-cycles all around me . . .'

He said gently: 'So you turned the car round, and in so doing mounted the kerb and hit a lamp-post.'

'Yes,' she said. 'I wasn't wearing my seat belt, and bumped my head. Not very hard, but it was the last straw. I fumbled the foot pedals. The engine stalled. I kept hearing the motor-cycles and knew I should never have time to start the engine, turn the car and get away. So I – I threw open the door and ran. Ran and ran. I think I must have been screaming then. After that, everything became darkness. Panic. An impulse to get away – anywhere. And it all ended in – nothing. There was this policeman asking me if I was ill, or if I had had an accident. And I couldn't think of anything to say. Or perhaps I couldn't remember. I don't know now.'

He reached and drew aside the sweep of dark hair that slanted across her right temple.

'I can see the mark where you struck your head,' he said. 'I wouldn't have thought it was enough to give you even a slight concussion. Did it knock you unconscious – even for a brief while?'

'I don't think so,' said Kate. 'No – I'm sure it didn't. There wasn't an instant's respite from the fear of those awful motor-cycles.

'No headache? But I asked you that when I saw you yesterday.'

'No.'

'Mmm. But there seems to be some loss of memory, though your other mental functions appear to be okay.' Again, he lifted her eyelids; but this time he shone a pencil torch into her pupils; brought his florid face so close to her face that she could smell the tang of after-shave on his skin. 'I wouldn't think there's any con-cussion,' he said, 'but, to be on the safe side, I'm in-clined to send you for some pictures and a few tests.' Taking a note-pad from his bag, he scribbled a few lines, folded up the sheet, placed it in an envelope and added an address. 'Go round to the Brompton Hospital this afternoon. Take a taxi. Don't drive. They'll attend to you. We can forget about the sleeping capsules, though I strongly advise you to have an early night and let Art with a capital A look after itself for a couple of days. And nights. Don't bother to get up, Mrs Hawks-moor, I'll let myself out. And I really do like your new painting.'

'Goodbye, Doctor – er . . .' She held out her hand.

'Manners,' he supplied. 'By the way, I had no idea that there was a child in the house. There was some confusion in everyone's mind, when I was here yester-day, about her – she is a girl? – her whereabouts. Now happily resolved, I suppose?'

The effect of this question upon Kate Hawksmoor was immediate and alarming. She jerked upright and fixed him with a wild-eyed stare.

'What do you mean by *that*?' she whispered. '*Have you*

been spying on me?'

'I – Mrs Hawksmoor, I don't know what to say . . .'

'Go away!' she cried, turning her head and burying her face against the suavely-cushioned back of the sofa.

'Mrs Hawksmoor . . .' The big, ruddy-faced, assured, rugger-playing medic was entirely put out of countenance.

'Why don't you leave me alone?' she cried. 'Why don't you all leave me alone? I only did what had to be done, sooner or later!'

CHAPTER IV

WORKING SWIFTLY, she heightened the mystery of the oval-shaped room by scraping away some of her scumble with the palette knife and revealing the dark underpaint. The outline of a shadow seemed now to be cast over the second, closed door which she was about to open . . .

I have always been a lonely, private sort of person; didn't make a single friend at the Royal College, but just crept into my corner where my easel was set up and got on with it, pausing only for sandwiches and a flask of coffee on the job.

Giles, for all his superficial extrovert manner, was as private as I, though he tried to fight it. He brought a few friends and acquaintances to the marriage: people from New-market, where he hunted about three times a year and some-times rode point-to-point without any notable success; his partners and their wives; two men he had been at school with. It was one of them who brought Zoë Chalmers to one of our rare cocktail-parties at the flat.

My only outward-looking activity was what Giles always referred to with gentle mockery as my 'do-goodery'.

He said: 'Darling, it's a puzzle to know if your liberal conscience stems from the influence of your father's socialism or from the traditional aristocratic taste for do-goodery that descended upon him when they made him a Lord.'

'My father,' I told him, 'was among the most uncharitable persons I have ever known in my life. Darling, would you

believe that, on flag days and poppy days, my father sallied forth wearing a flag or poppy from a previous year, from a collection that he kept in a drawer?'

We both laughed at that. Poor father; poor, earnest, humourless Dad; for ever condemned by his poverty-stricken childhood in a mining village to suffer agonies of conscience about turtle soup at mayoral banquets; loveless in marriage and finding a furtive release, after Mother's death, with ladies of the night.

'However,' said Giles, 'your present interesting condition, my darling, is greatly going to curtail your charitable works. And I must say you look delicious in that little number you have on.'

'This little number I have on,' I informed him, 'is a very clever little number that hides a multitude of sins. Giles darling, if we are to have another party, let it be soon, before Pussy gets too prominent.'

'You are quite convinced she's to be a girl, aren't you?'

'Totally convinced. She is a girl. She will be named Priscilla and called Pussy.'

I was in my fourth month and everything was going fine. I even drove the Rolls down to Goudley to see Nannie, whom we had established in a weekend cottage that Giles had inherited from his brother's estate. Nannie Porter had been nursemaid to both Giles and Joe, and – perhaps sensing in me someone who had never really learned to cope with the knocks of life – had adopted me, from the first, as one of her 'charges'. It was arranged that she would come to the London flat and be with me at the birth and for as long afterwards as she chose.

The party – which Giles called: 'The Pre-Coming-out Party' – was a long way short of a howling success. The caterers we had arranged to come in got the wrong night; I deiced the fridge by mistake and there was no ice for the drinks. The affair would have been a disaster if it had been left to me: all I wanted to do was run away, hide in a dark corner and put my fingers in my ears. It was Zoë Chalmers who saved the evening. Poised, capable Zoë sent a man out to a local hotel to beg, borrow or steal ice; under her direction, the womenfolk turned to and cut sandwiches, made rudimentary canapés from bits and pieces of cold stuff I had around the place; and all the time she controlled the enterprise with the cool and unflappable expertise of an ace military commander. How I envied her for her fortitude, as I envied her for her hair, which was of that crisp blonde kind that just needs the fingers to be run through it on rising, and the sort of complexion which puts one in mind of ski slopes in the Alpine sun.

The party over, the guests gone, Giles and I were getting ready for bed.

'Thank God for Zoë,' said Giles. 'That girl worked like a beaver and saved the situation.'

'Without detracting one iota from my indebtedness to Zoë,' I replied snappily, 'I would point out that she never so much as soiled her hands with a bread-knife, nor touched a washing-up cloth when it was all over.'

'She certainly got the other girls moving,' he replied. 'Jolly capable girl.'

'Capable of anything,' was my tart reply.

'Kate, that's unfair,' he said. 'And quite unworthy of you.'

'I am an unworthy person,' I said, knowing as I said it that I was seeking out trouble – and not caring. 'Not the sort to inspire your commendation and admiration. Unlike Zoë Chalmers.'

'Kate, what are you getting at?'

I rounded on him. 'Oh, come, let's not be naïve, darling. You were throwing hot glances at her all evening, and she was throwing them right back. Everyone else noticed your carrying-on, why should you suppose I didn't?'

He would not fight me, badly as I wanted him to; instead of reacting with anger, or contempt, or incredulity, he simply came over to where I was sitting on the edge of the bed, put his hands on my shoulders.

'Cheer up, kiddo,' he said. 'It's been a bloody awful evening for you, but it's all over now.'

'Oh, Giles!' I clung to him. 'I'm so fed up. Most of the time it's fine, but sometimes it gets me down. I feel so clumsy, so ugly, sometimes. Other times, I feel like a sacred vessel. This wasn't one of my sacred vessel nights. And then along comes Zoë Chalmers, all sun-kissed and bloody capable. I hate the bitch.'

'Well, I promise you I wasn't treating her to hot glances, darling,' he said. 'Scout's honour.'

'That you mayn't have,' I conceded. 'But she was sending plenty in your direction, chum!'

Later, lying together in the darkness with his arm about me, I rebuked myself for the scene I had created, and rejoiced in thanks for the way which he had charmed away my malaise. And I thought of my great happiness. To be in love and to be loved. To be bearing his child . . .

The second door was opened wide. Set against the blue sky was her – Kate Hawksmoor's – head, drawn and painted to the same large proportion as its companion in the adjacent doorway. Coloured for happiness.

But in the sky above and beyond – a small cloud no bigger than a hand.

The cemetery was only four blocks from Kate's flat. She parked the Rolls-Royce close by the gates, in between two other cars, aligning herself with the kerb only after the third shot, and then touching bumpers; so that she was breathless and trembling with the nervous effort when she got out. Fortunately no one – and particularly not the owner of the other car – had witnessed her exhibition.

The early morning sun, which had promised an un-clouded day, had long hidden itself in drifting greyness, and a faint feathering of thin rain met her as she went in through the gates. She dug her hands deeply into the pockets of her mackintosh, bowed her head, and walked swiftly down the path leading to the heart of the cemetery.

She had been there only twice before, but was able to find the grave without the slightest difficulty: a simple marble headstone, inscribed with her dead husband's name and dates. A posy of immortelles stood under a dusty glass dome. Grass was growing in some abandonment round the base of the stone. Kate knelt in the dampness and started to pull it away, tuft by tuft, thinking all the time that, try as she might, she could not encompass the memory of the man she had known and loved as Giles Hawksmoor within the limits of a plot of ground eight feet by four, nor reduce everything Giles had been – and still remained – to the arbitrary date that recorded his passing. It was for this reason that she had visited the grave only twice in three years: the pilgrimage was, quite simply, without meaning or significance. Giles Hawksmoor's poor remains might lie in London clay, but all that mattered about Giles Hawksmoor lived on, still, in the repository of her own mind.

Today, she had hoped for something more. As if Giles – that secret part of Giles which existed outside her own mind and her own experience of him – would speak out from the London clay and augment her memories of him. The painting of the oval-shaped room with its five secret doors had captured her total attention, to the exclusion of all else. Since revealing to herself the content of the first two doors, she had lived in an agony of apprehension. The third door beckoned to be opened; she would almost certainly be compelled to take up her brushes and palette the moment she returned home. The prospect terrified her.

The last of the coarse grass that had grown up round the base of the headstone lay in a small heap. It seemed churlish to throw it in the path, worse still to put it on someone else's plot. Kate settled for cramming it into the pocket of her mackintosh. In the act of so doing, she became aware that an old man in a peaked cap, some kind of cemetery attendant, was watching her from behind the statue of an angel bearing in its marble arms a dead baby. With a guilty start, she withdrew the handful of grass and laid it contritely in front of Giles Hawksmoor's headstone.

The old attendant limped out from behind the

statue and made some play of stabbing at the ground
with a pin on the end of a stick, till this activity brought
him closer to the kneeling woman.

' 'Afternoon,' he said.

'Good afternoon,' responded Kate hastily.

'Nasty bit of ole rain,' he said.

'Yes,' she whispered.

'Mind you, we can't complain,' he said. 'And the
gardeners want it.'

'Yes.'

He nodded, casting a rheumy eye at the pile of
plucked coarse grass lying in front of the headstone
close by her knee. He shuffled off; had not gone more
than a few paces before he turned.

'Friend o' yours, is he?'

'I'm sorry,' faltered Kate. 'What did you say?'

'That feller over there.' He made a brief stab with his
spiked stick. 'Feller over by the trees. Followed you in.
Been watchin' you ever since you came in, he has.'

'Watching me?' She felt her mouth and throat suddenly go dry.

'The dark-lookin' feller. Thought he might be your
hubby or somethin'.' The old man laughed, coughed.
'Just thought I'd mention it in passing, like. Never had
much education myself,' he added inconsequentially.

Kate watched the old man pick his way between the
graves, stabbing here and there as he went, till his
slight figure disappeared from her sight; and then,
slowly, fearfully, she turned her gaze in the direction to
which her informant had pointed her. A hundred – a
hundred and fifty – yards from where she knelt, was a

copse of cypresses, green and shimmering in the rain. In the centre of the clump, in the most shaded part, stood a tall man whose face was not entirely obscured by shadow.

Dark. Dark as an Arab . . .

She was on her feet in the instant.

'Go away!' she screamed. 'Leave me alone!'

Appalled by her audacity, she all but turned and ran; but an imp of caution warned her that her mysterious watcher barred her way to the gates, and to attempt escape in the opposite direction was to commit herself to the inner labyrinth of the cemetery and give her watcher the opportunity to turn pursuer. Necessity dictated that she must stand her ground. It was an option that tested her screaming nerve ends to breaking-point – when the man in the clump of cypresses straightened himself, took a hand out of a pocket, and began to walk towards her, picking his way carefully in and out of the grave plots.

Kate awaited his coming, her breath quickening.

'Mrs Hawksmoor. Er – good day.'

She managed to mouth the words: 'Good day.'

'Forgive me for intruding. I saw that you were tending a grave, and realized that it was most thoughtless of me to follow you in here. I should have waited by the car till you came out.'

'Who – who are you?' she breathed.

He was no Arab; merely bronzed by some alien sun. His eyes were cornflower blue. Hair raven black with deep blue lights.

'My name's Carter. Jock Carter,' he said. 'You don't

know me from Adam, Mrs Hawksmoor, but I'm
interested in the car, you know.'

'The car?' She stared at him wonderingly.

'The Rolls. The garage gave me your address and
phone number. Advised me to get in touch with you
direct. I must say it's in very lovely condition. When
did you get the slight dent in the front? Not that it
matters. Quite easily straightened out.'

Kate had the distinct impression of reality receding
from her till it was as if she and the stranger had no
physical substance, and both of them, and the bizarre
surroundings of the sleeping dead, existed only as a
half-formed thought in her own mind; notwithstanding
which, she made a determined attempt to retain her
grip upon the here and now.

She said: 'Please, Mr Er . . .'

'Carter,' he supplied, grinning to show very good
teeth.

'Mr Carter, I simply don't know what you're talking
about.'

He looked disappointed. 'Oh, don't tell me I've got
it wrong,' he said. 'Surely you *are* Mrs Hawksmoor, and
you *did* ask the garage the other day, when your Rolls
was in for servicing, if they'd put it up for sale?'

'For sale? Oh . . .'

(Think, girl. Think. When was the car in for servicing? Was it yesterday – last week? Yes, I did have
some notion about selling it. God, what's happening to
my memory? This man will think I'm insane . . .)

He was watching her intently, the blue eyes searching
her expression, mouth waiting to grin or to express dis-

may – depending upon her answer.

'Perhaps you've changed your mind, Mrs Hawks-moor.'

'Oh, no!' she blurted out the declaration.

'Then I'm in the running as a possible purchaser?' The blue eyes danced eagerly. 'I'll top any offer you've had already.'

'I haven't had any other offer,' she said.

Carter spread his hands. 'Then you have a sale, Mrs Hawksmoor,' he declared. 'Name your price.'

Bemused, Kate said: 'I've really no idea what a Rolls is worth. My – my late husband dealt with all that.'

(What an absurd statement. Absurd, also, to gesture towards the headstone. 'Meet my hubby, Mr Carter.' God, I *am* going mad!)

'May I make a suggestion?' he said. 'Here's what we do . . .'

'Water or soda?'

'Spot of water, please,' said Carter.

She had fallen in with his suggestion, which was that they return to her place, where she would phone the garage and ask them to advise on a price for the Rolls. The garage had obligingly indicated the sum of £16,000, to which Carter had agreed without batting an eyelid; had produced a cheque-book and written out a cheque for the amount. It was now half past one. Kate, who felt that she should be offering him lunch (since, like her, he clearly had not eaten), compromised by giving him a drink. It seemed barely civil; and all she wanted was for him to go away and leave her alone.

'Cheers,' he said, raising the whisky glass.

'Your very good health,' murmured Kate.

'You're not joining me.'

'I seldom drink,' she said truthfully.

He took a swallow. 'Tell you what I'll do,' he said. 'I'll drop the cheque into your bank before they close this afternoon and ask them to advise us both as soon as it's been cleared. To tell the truth, I'd very much hoped to have had the motor-car for the weekend. You'd scarcely believe this, Mrs Hawksmoor, but I've lived and breathed, eaten and slept with the idea of a motor-car like that Rolls all through the last five years of driving beaten-up old rattletraps all over the dirt roads of Queensland. Can you wonder I drove after you when I saw you going out? Sorry I alarmed you in the cemetery, though.'

'You can take the car,' she said. 'Straight away. Now.'

(Anything to get rid of him. This is a man who's limbering up to tell me his life-story.)

He shook his head. 'Hell, no, Mrs Hawksmoor,' he said. 'You can't go round trusting wild colonial boys who come offering you joke cheques in exchange for Rolls-Royces. I couldn't let you do it, ma'am. I'm a big boy now, and I can wait in patience till the cheque clears. Tell you what, though. I'd like to drop by some time over the weekend and gloat over my new baby. Promise I won't bother you. I won't even ring the doorbell.'

She nodded agreement. He had finished his drink and there was no alternative but to offer him another – which he accepted. Then they were thrown back on conversation again.

'Very nice place you've got here, Mrs Hawksmoor,' he said. 'Do you live here on your own? Excuse my asking, but I gathered from the garage that you are a widow.'

'I – I live here with my young daughter.' Her fingernails tensed against the chair arms. 'She – she's staying with a friend in the country.'

'I'm unmarried myself,' said Carter. 'But I love kids.'

She said hastily: 'And from Australia, I understand? From Queensland. Have you just arrived in England, Mr Carter?' She stole a sidelong glance at her elegant marble and ormolu clock that ticked thinly on the carved pearwood chimneypiece in the corner of the studio: 1.45 – did this man never eat?

She closed her mind, listened with her ears and looked in upon herself, aware that, far off, was a man who, indeed, had landed in the Old Country only a week ago, having spent five years sheep-farming with his brother in Queensland; had now sold out his share to the brother and was aiming to buy a farm in Devon or Cornwall. Did she know Devon and Cornwall? Yes, she knew both a little.

An introspective disposition, allied to childhood experience with parents with whom she had always found difficulty in communicating, had developed in Kate the facility of listening and carrying on a desultory conversation while at the same time looking around inside her head.

Mouthing platitudes about the West Country, she nagged her mind, meanwhile, about the memory lapse concerning the Rolls. Of course, she *had* instructed the garage to put the car on the market for her. Was there anything else, she asked herself, that she had done and forgotten?

Merciful heaven, he had at last drained his glass and was rising to go. A wave of gratitude mixed with remorse swept aside all else. After all, he had, without the slightest suggestion of haggling, paid over what must certainly be a very keen price for the Rolls. And she supposed he was quite a nice person. Indeed, any other woman but she would find him rather attractive, perhaps.

'Goodbye,' she said, extending her hand. 'And thank you so much for taking the Rolls off my hands. I shall be much happier with a small car.'

'It's you who deserves the thanks, Kate,' he said, squeezing her hand.

Striving to recall how and when they had slipped into first name terms, Kate opened the door for him. His car – a hired car, as he had explained when they had left the cemetery together in convoy – cringed beside the Rolls like a mongrel dog sucking up to a lordly Saluki.

'Well, goodbye, er – Jock,' she murmured.

'And mind you take no notice of me if I turn up on Saturday or Sunday,' he cautioned her. 'I'll just be running my hands along her bonnet and laughing to think of my brother Frank who's bouncing around in

an old utility truck down under.' He paused. The regarding blue eyes searched hers. 'Mind if I ask you
something personal, Kate?'

She gave a start of alarm that he could not but have
noticed.

'Why, of course not,' she said.

'Is anything the matter?'

'Matter?' She felt a surge of panic, and her gorge rose
with it.

'Something troubling you. I know it's none of my
business, but I have a very clear impression that you've
got some kind of worry on your mind. Hit me if I'm
wrong. Tell me to mind my own damned business.
But if there's anything I can do to help.' He grinned.
'Jock Carter – fixer. Specialist with damsels in distress.'

'No, it's nothing,' she said. 'It's just that I'm not – '
Her mind struggled to assemble a formula that would
encapsulate the hideous events with which she was
surrounded – 'I'm going through rather a bad time.'

His open, handsome, guileless face turned beetroot
red on the instant. The frank, regarding eyes sought
escape.

'Forgive me for asking – er – Kate,' he said. 'Well,
thanks for the drinks and thanks for everything. 'Bye.'

She closed the door upon him; leaned back against it
with a sigh of release. Hardly had his car moved out of
the drive and out of earshot when the phone rang.
Kate eyed it for a few moments of indecision, till
curiosity prompted her to lift the receiver.

'Hello,' she murmured, reluctant to announce her
number.

'Is Mrs Hawksmoor, please?'

The Arab! The veritable Arab, not to be confused with Mr Jock Carter, late of Queensland, Australia. And was he, after all, as innocuous as Jock Carter? She had to know.

'Who is calling?' she asked guardedly.

'Madam, I am secretary to His Excellency the Sheik Abdul Ali Mansour, who is living in The Boltons quite near to you. His Excellency has instructed me to obtain Rolls-Royce, and I telephoned garage, who informed me . . .'

She had an impulse to giggle. It really was farcical. To have set in motion a train of events – and yet to have no recollection of having done so. Farcical – and alarming.

She broke through the Arab's diatribe: 'I am terribly sorry, but the car is already sold.'

'Please, has transaction been completed? Money is no object. His Excellency will better any price you have been . . .'

'The car is sold,' said Kate firmly. 'Goodbye.'

She replaced the receiver. Turning, she met the eyes of the child in the painting. The one standing against the wall; not the mysterious composition upon which she was presently engaged. The wistful eyes spoke out to her.

'I have to go through with it, Pussy,' she whispered. 'Right through to the end – no matter how much it hurts.'

CHAPTER V

THE THIRD DOOR, which she was now about to open, lay in deep shadow. She squeezed fresh worms of bright paint on to the smooth mahogany of her palette; steeled herself to fling open the door and allow the searching daylight of memory to illuminate the agony that lay beyond . . .

We had only one visitor after the awful party, and that was months later. Cynthia Brierley caught me unawares one morning while I was painting. I think that, forewarned, I would have pretended to be out, but she saw me at the studio window, when, hearing her car's tyres crunching up the gravel drive, I went to peer out and see who it was.

'You're looking simply super, dear,' she told me falsely. 'Still hardly showing at all. When's the great day?'

'Three weeks,' I told her, covertly glancing at my picture, on which I had been tackling a particularly difficult and absorbingly interesting passage when she had disturbed me.

'How's Giles?'

'Working very hard.' (And so am I, so for heaven's sake drink up your nice tea and push off!)

'Will he be home soon? I should love to see him. It's been so long.'

'No. He's away.' I explained how the firm, in common with so many others, had found overheads in the City so impossible that they had recently hived off a large part of the administrative and office staff and set them up in premises in Plymouth. Of

late, Giles had taken to driving down to Plymouth at least once a week and stopping overnight.

To my relief, Cynthia did not stay long after that. I had the wry impression that she had only called by to make sure that my pregnancy was still a going concern – and that the confirmation of same was, to her, a matter for some regret. I recalled Giles trying to explain to me once about the niceties of his family estate, and how it was that, if he had remained a bachelor, the odious Brierleys would have stood to inherit everything in the event of his death.

'Not all your beauty and talent, nor your adorable disposition and exquisite bosom,' he had grinningly informed me, 'but the prospect of you and your progeny putting old Col and old Cynth's noses out of joint made me press my suit with you, darling.'

Cynthia called on a Thursday. I slept alone in the flat that night, not unduly put out because Giles did not ring me in the evening from Plymouth, as he did more often than not. I was exceedingly tired, for I had never got the hang of being able to paint sitting down. Pussy was very lively that night, and I was a long time in getting to sleep. It seemed only a minute before I was blinking at the early morning sunlight streaming in through the gauzy curtains of my bedroom, with the ring of the doorbell still echoing in my ears.

I knew something was wrong – terribly and hideously wrong – before even I looked out and saw the police car parked in the drive, with the man at the wheel sitting there and idly tapping the sill of his door. And then the bell sounded again.

Pulling my dressing-gown over my shoulders, I went on down; half of my mind telling me to run, the other trying to hold me back – to protract the fast disappearing moments of ignorance and speculation that were my only barriers against awful truth.

'Mrs Hawksmoor, is it – Mrs Giles Hawksmoor?'

She was a pleasant-faced, dumpy little woman in her late forties, dressed in a sensible grey costume, sensible stockings, flat-heeled shoes. I suppose she was employed specifically for the job of bearing news to shatter people's lives. It must be a rotten job to hold down.

I stammered a question. Yes, it was Giles. Not hurt. Killed.

Next, I remember sitting in the armchair in the studio, with the plainclothes police lady making me a nice hot cup of tea and trying to perform the impossible feat of softening the blow, while at the same time regaling me with the most excruciatingly hideous details.

Was there someone – some friend or relation I could go to? Not to Mr and Mrs Brierley; they had gone down to Cornwall, formally to identify the body, which had just been recovered. They, the police, would happily provide a driver for my own car and take me anywhere I wished to go. Should she send for my doctor? In my condition, it would best be wise than sorry. Such a terrible thing to happen at such a time. When was the baby due?

It must have been then that I screamed and threw the nice hot cup of tea at the far wall. After that, it was a silent moving picture in sepia, with me in the front row of the stalls: the road rolling up like a ribbon of sunlight in front of us; a stranger in a peaked cap in the driving seat; a numb feeling where my mind had been.

I cried for the first time when I saw Nannie's wise, pippin-cheeked countenance and felt her skinny arms about me. She put

me to bed in the room at the back of the cottage in Goudley that
had big pink cabbage roses on the wallpaper. Whatever it was
they had given me that had turned my conscious existence into
a silent moving picture then let go of me, and I fell, spinning,
tumbling, turning, into a blessed oblivion.

I marvel at the unexpected depths of resilience in other
people; how much more surprising when it springs, all un-
bidden, from oneself. Later – days later, but how many days
later I have no way of telling and have never enquired about – I
was able to question Nannie as to the details of the tragedy. The
poor old soul did the best she was able with the grim material
she had to hand. Yes, Giles was now buried. In Brompton
cemetery . . .

How had it happened?

More at home with the cosy subject of interment than with
the circumstances and appurtenances of violent death, Nannie's
account became more stark, less particular as to details. Giles's
car had fallen down a cliff in Cornwall.

In Cornwall?

Yes, and he in it. Death must have been instantaneous, for so
the doctor had said at the inquest, and that was a blessing.

But how – how?

An accident, they said. He must have driven his sports car off
the road to admire the view (it had been a moonlit night and the
place was a favoured beauty spot – these facts I gleaned later,
from newspaper reports, not from poor Nannie), and forgot to
put on the brake.

But – why Cornwall?

No one – and Nannie Porter least of all – ever provided me
with the answer to that. It was assumed – and I assumed it
also – that Giles, following a hard day at the branch office in

Plymouth, had taken off on an impulse; driving westwards in the sunny summer's evening, the hood of his Aston let down and his hair streaming; 'burning up the miles' – as he was so fond of putting it. There was no trace of his progress along the way, no record of his having called in at any pub or hotel. A wall of nothingness lay across the final journey of Giles Hawksmoor, that ended with a crumpled sports car and its dead driver at the cliff bottom.

I marvelled then, and I marvel still, at my resilience. It was I who took matters firmly in hand; Nannie was only a numbly acquiescent handmaiden to my designs, gazing at me with red-rimmed, tearful eyes clouded with wonder and disbelief to see how her protégée, her helpless and indecisive grown-up child, had so blossomed in adversity. We would stay in Goudley for the birth, I told her. My child – Giles's daughter – was not going to start life in smoky old London – not she. That precious life, my only living connection with my dead husband and lover, would first see light in the peace and tranquillity of rural Kent, with the heady scent of the hop-fields drifting in through the leaded lights and the sound of bees in the tall hollyhocks by our pebble-dashed wall.

And so I allowed myself to drift through languid and empty days in our tiny cottage garden, reclining upon a wicker arm-chair with a huge red and yellow umbrella shading me and my book. I read a lot, that is to say I was frequently to be seen with a book in my lap; but in the last days of my pregnancy I never progressed beyond the opening pages of the novel; my whole attention, the focus of my entire being, was directed upon the living child who moved beneath my heart. For the first time since her conception, my body became, and constantly remained, that very 'sacred vessel'. I would lie and glory in the wonder of joys that were daily coming nearer to the reach of my eager fingertips. Giles, the man I had loved with all my heart, was taken from me. The insupportable had to be borne – must be borne, and would be borne – and only through the coming of our child.

Priscilla, my darling Pussy, was coming to me. The encounter was to be, in part, a reunion with my dead Giles. Through her, the quenched flame of his life was to burn forth anew and fill my world with glorious light.

And so the sunny summer days drifted past. Nannie was well satisfied with my condition, and smilingly assured me that all would be well. She chivvied and bullied the doctor from Tunbridge Wells: a bland and shuffling old fellow who persisted in addressing me as 'dear lady' and allowed me to listen to Pussy's heartbeats through his stethoscope. With some reluctance – for I had set my heart upon my child being born in the room with the pink cabbage rose wallpaper (which had been Giles's and my room) – I agreed to go into a nursing home at Tunbridge Wells for the delivery. The cottage did not have a phone but there was a public call-box in the village, and the local taxi had been alerted for call on a twenty-four-hour-a-day basis. In the happy event, my heart's desire came true, the taxi remained uncalled, the bed in the nursing home unused.

My daughter confounded all their designs by making her unannounced appearance in the early hours of the morning. At the first tokens of her coming, I called out for Nannie, who was sleeping in the next room with her door propped open in anticipation of just such an eventuality. Guided by her soothing voice, allowing myself willingly to obey her, I passed through the unbelievable and strange agonies and out into the bliss of deliverance; till, weary beyond all understanding, I reached out

*to take the small, pink scrap of new life from Nannie's arms,
the question trembling on my lips.*

Yes, it was a girl. A lovely little girl . . .

The third door stood open. It revealed a landscape
that was distanced by receding planes of green meadows,
fields tall with ripe hops, oast houses — the landscape
of rural Kent. In the middle ground, the figure of a man
was about to enter a winding lane that led into a tunnel
of dark greenery. The traveller looked back over his
shoulder with an expression of wistful regret that con-
tained a hint of a secret joy. It was Giles Hawksmoor.

Close in the foreground, a naked new-born baby girl
lay, kicking and crowing with delight, in a patch of
sunlight. Just as Kate Hawksmoor remembered her on
the night of her birth, when she had delighted in the
warmth and sweetness that she had held against her
breast in the room with the pink cabbage rose wallpaper
those three years before in Goudley.

For the past two days Kate had been existing on scraps
from the fridge. It was dusk – a magical, pinky-violet
summer's sundown, smelling of honeysuckle – when she
laid aside her brushes and snatched a cat nap on the
studio sofa. Awakening, she went to the fridge; spread
the last of a very dried-up paté on an oatmeal biscuit,
poured herself a glass of milk, and took them back into
the studio. And the phone rang.

Another candidate for the Rolls! Taking a sip of
milk, she picked up the receiver.

'I'm very sorry, but the car is already sold.'

'Is that you, Kate dear? It's Cynth. What was that

you said about a car?'

Cynthia Brierley! Hope to heaven she isn't inviting herself round again!

'It was nothing, Cynthia,' she said. 'How are you?'

'How are *you*, more like? We've been worried out of our minds for you, duckie. I tried to phone several times, but got no answer.'

'I – I haven't been answering the phone much,' said Kate feebly.

'But you're feeling better?'

'Much better, thanks. I – went out today.'

'Well, that's fine. Making the best of the lovely weather.'

'It rained.'

'Ah, but it's cleared up now. We had supper out on the patio and it could have been Marbella or Alicante. And that's why I'm ringing you, dear. The weather report for tomorrow's a heatwave, so no matter what you say Col and I are going down to fetch darling Priscilla from Goudley.'

'*No-o-o!*'

'It'll be no trouble at all, Kate dear.' The mincing, careful voice was dangerously firm. 'We'll go down first thing in the morning and bring the little mite back here, so she can play in the pool.'

'She – she doesn't like swimming!' Kate blurted the first objection that sprang to her mind.

'No need to swim. She can splash about and play on the water chute. She'll love it.' There was a hard edge of determination in Cynthia's manner that stemmed, surely, from something more than an impulse to make a small child happy.

'Cynthia, please, I'd much rather you left Pussy with Nannie.' Kate caught her reflection in the mirror opposite. Her eyes were haunted. 'Please, I really would.'

'Nonsense, dear,' came the response. 'It would be the height of selfishness to leave an active kiddie to spend a glorious weekend like we're going to have in a pokey little cottage garden with an old woman. I'll not hear any more arguments, dear. Just leave everything to Col and me.'

'Cynthia . . .'

'That's all right, dear. Put your mind at rest and concentrate on getting well. Have you fixed for someone to come in and help yet?'

'Not yet. I . . .'

'Well, see that you fix it tomorrow. 'Bye for now, dear. I'll give your love to little Priscilla.'

The phone went dead.

The glass of milk fell, unregarded, from Kate's nerveless fingers as she slowly sank to the floor and buried her face in her hands.

'Oh, God, why did it have to happen like this? Why did it have to end so – messily?'

At nine o'clock next morning, Colin and Cynthia Brierley were driving through Kent's tree-shaded lanes and indulging in what promised to develop into one of their habitual nagging rows.

'If you hadn't played ducks and drakes with your life – and with *my* life – we wouldn't be in the position of having to suck up to that snobby bitch!' Cynthia's nose went pinched and red when she was angry – a fact that her husband registered, with the usual twinge of distaste, in his rear-view mirror.

'For a look-in on half a million quid, I don't call being civil to my cousin's widow sucking up.' An ex-minor public school man, Brierley did not ascribe the patrician quality of civility to his wife; the nearest she got to it was what she called 'politeness'.

'Fat chance *you* have of seeing anything of that kind of money,' retorted Cynthia scornfully. 'The loan of a tenner now and again is all you'll get out of the Honourable Kate.'

'I have every hope of raising a very considerable sum, and that soon,' said Brierley. And he added something under his breath.

Cynthia caught it – or some of it. She leapt upon it like a dog upon a bone.

'What was that you said?' she shrilled. 'Something about: "God help us all if I don't"? Is that what you said?'

'And if I did?' he demanded challengingly.

'Colin Brierley, what have you been up to now, you bastard?'

'Bloody shut up, woman!'

'You're in trouble again!' she shouted. 'I knew it! I've been suspecting it for weeks. You've been drinking like a fish. You always drink like a fish just before the crash comes. *And* I'd bet you've got *yet* another woman in tow. Who is she *this* time? And what have you been at?'

'Shut up, damn you!'

'I was right!' Bright red spots on the cheekbones now vied in hue with the discoloration of her nose. 'You've been on the crook again!'

' "On the crook." ' He sneered. 'At what street corner did you pick up all these quaintly proletarian expressions?'

She swore and struck him. The car swerved wildly across the road. Mounted the far bank. He jammed on the brake. The engine choked. Died.

'Christ, I'll do porridge for you one day, damn me if I won't!' he shouted.

She wiped his spittle from her face. She was smiling now: a tight, triumphant smile.

' "Do porridge." ' she said. '*Now* who's using quaintly proletarian expressions?'

He slapped her across the mouth.

She scarcely flinched. Her eyes never left his as she wearily wiped a thin trail of blood from her lips.

'You really are up to your eyes in it, aren't you?' she said. 'What is it this time? Had to kill somebody to keep them quiet about one of your charming little schemes that always seem to blow up in your face?'

His fury had subsided against the force of her cold contempt.

'It's going to be all right,' he said. 'Nothing's happened that money can't solve. Plenty of money. And Kate's my only hope. All you have to do is string along with me and don't ask questions.'

'I don't have any choice, do I?' she said. 'Eight of the best years of my life I've given to you. I'm not going to let it all go – the house, the pool, the patio and everything – for you to hand it all over to some young scrubber. That would be just like you.'

'All right.' He was past arguing any further. 'Let's get this show on the road, then.'

He took off the hand-brake and restarted the engine. Driving slowly – for the swerve into the far bank had severely taxed his nerves – they came at length to the pleasant village of Goudley, which consists of a twelfth-century church with very fine brasses and a reputed sword of King Edward III, a post office and general store, a Tudor manor house, Edwardian vicarage with immemorial cedars, twenty or so cottages of excellent Kentish slate and flint, a village green dominated by a war memorial dating from World War I.

'The cottage is the long one on the other side of the green,' said Brierley. 'I only went there once in my life. My well-off cousins were not encouraged to mix with little Colin a great deal, and the habit stuck when Joe and Giles grew up.'

His wife did not reply; she was not in a replying frame of mind; nor did she get out of the car when Brierley went to knock at the front door of the cottage. She was powdering her nose when he came back. His face was puzzled.

'That's funny,' he said.

'It'll be the first funny thing that's happened today,' was her tart retort.

'There's no one at home,' he said. 'Furthermore, there are dust covers over all the furniture. I looked in through the window. It's as if . . .'

'It's as if – *what*?' she demanded shrilly.

'Why, as if there's no one living at the place.'

'There *has* to be someone living there!' she cried. 'The old woman's living there, isn't she? And the kid's staying there with her, isn't she?'

'Then why . . .?'

'Why? Well, I s'pose that, being old and past it, the old girl's closed down most of the rooms that she doesn't use. Go round to the back door. You'll probably find that she mostly lives in the kitchen.'

A young boy was cycling along the path that skirted the green. A newspaper lad: there was a canvas bag slung on the bike's handlebars. He rode straight to pass by the Brierleys – and past the cottage – without stopping. Colin Brierley called after him:

'Hey, sonny – Miss Porter?'

'Huh?'

'Miss Porter – is she in, do you know?'

The youth stopped his bike; looked at Brierley in puzzlement.

'Not Miss Porter,' he said.

'Why not?'

'Why, Miss Porter, she's dead.'

'*Dead*?'

'Died a year or so since. And her sister.'

There was a telephone-box at the far side of the green. The Brierleys went to it immediately after leaving the churchyard, where they had confirmed with their own astounded eyes the truth of the newslad's assertion: Emily Jane Porter had departed this life on 15 February two years previously; she shared her final resting place with a Gertrude Maude Fox, née Porter, who had joined her there two months later.

'Who're you going to ring?' cried Cynthia.

'Kate, of course,' retorted her husband.

'What's the use? You'll get nothing from her. Nothing but lies!' Cynthia was teetering on the edge of hysteria. 'We've got to do something, and fast. I don't trust that cow. Remember how she tried to keep us away from here? Where's that kiddie? that's what I want to know. Here – gimme that phone!'

She wrenched the receiver from her husband's hand and dialled 999 for the police.

CHAPTER VI

IMMEDIATELY upon his arrival in his office that morning, Detective Chief Superintendent Alex Cushman, who was senior Duty Officer, was visited by his principal assistant.

Detective-Inspector Mark Orville stood six feet four inches and had to stoop to get in the door. Cushman, who was a man of tidy, not to say pernickety, personal habits, always experienced a frisson of anxiety when his junior swayed dangerously close to the chimneypiece, upon which stood a pair of exquisite Meissen figures representing Tragedy and Comedy – both of them slightly damaged, as was most of Cushman's Meissen collection. He bought sparingly and prudently from country sales, and the salary of a policeman does not run to the assembling of the perfect.

'Well?' Cushman watched anxiously as the younger man safely negotiated the proximity of the chimneypiece and coiled his great length upon a chair facing his chief. 'Anything interesting in overnight?'

Orville's long face betrayed no animation as he riffled through the pages of a notebook.

'Nothing much, sir,' he said. 'A break-in, but nothing taken. Accident in Kensington High Street. The car was abandoned afterwards, so the driver was either drunk and avoiding the breathalyser, or it's a hot car. And there's a suspected missing child.'

'Hardly the sort of fare to justify dragging me away from my garden on a day like this,' said Cushman, taking out his pipe and tobacco. 'All nicely in hand, I suppose?'

'Yes, sir,' said Orville, eyeing his chief's pipe with distaste. 'But I'd like your opinion on the missing child.'

'That's what I'm here for, Mark,' said the other, puffing contentedly, wryly aware that smoking was an anathema to his gangling assistant, who was a keep-fit buff and winner for three years in succession of the 1500-metres race at the Metropolitan Police Athletics.

'We had a call just after nine, from a phone-box in Goudley, Kent.'

'I know it well,' said Cushman. 'Went to a farm sale near there last year and picked up a very fine *épergne*, almost perfect, very cheaply. Go on.'

'A couple, name of Brierley, reported that they were down there to pick up a child – Priscilla Hawksmoor, aged three, the daughter of Mr Brierley's late cousin – at the instigation of the mother, who told them the child was staying with the old retired family nursemaid. Upon arrival at Goudley, the Brierleys were surprised to learn that the old woman, Emily Porter, died two years ago.'

'I'll bet they were surprised,' said Cushman. 'That's a very rum thing.'

'I thought so, too, sir,' said Orville. 'Then the name Hawksmoor rang a bell and I remembered an incident earlier in the week. I checked back. Early Thursday morning, it was.' He glanced at his notebook. 'A Mrs Kate Hawksmoor was picked up wandering in the

King's Road in a dazed condition. She was identified from the contents of her handbag, which are listed here. There was a garage receipt for the servicing of a Rolls-Royce, which connected her with a Rolls that had been found piled up against a lamp-post in Hammersmith earlier that night.'

'She had a shunt, got concussed, is that it?'

'That's about the size of it, I reckon,' said Orville.

'And this is the same woman who told the – what was their name? – Brierleys that her kid was staying with the old woman at Goudley?'

'Yes, sir. It was the Brierleys who were sent for when Mrs Hawksmoor was taken home. The officer told off to look after her found them in an address book there. They're the only living relatives.'

'Well, then,' said Cushman, 'it looks as if we have a simple case of loss of memory following concussion. Mrs Hawksmoor sent her child away to stay with friends. During a temporary loss of memory following her shunt, she mistakenly informed the Brierleys that the child was with the dead nursemaid. Was a doctor brought in?'

'Dr Manners, sir,'

'Well, get on to Dr Manners. He's a level-headed sort of chap, and no nonsense. Ask him to confirm the concussion angle. After that, go round and see Mrs Hawksmoor yourself. If she's still at home, that is. She may have gone to her child.'

'I telephoned her as soon as I had the call from the Brierleys, sir. No reply.'

'Did the Brierleys have the same experience? Surely they must have rung her first off.'

'They didn't say, sir.'

'Mmm.' Cushman frowned thoughtfully. 'Hawksmoor – not a commonplace name. Rings a bell with me, too. Do we have anything else on file?'

'I was coming to that, sir,' replied Orville.

Cushman snapped his fingers. 'Hawksmoor! That was the name of the half-wit who tried to do a double circumnavigation single-handed and disappeared without trace. Any relation?'

Orville pouted like a small boy who has had his catapult confiscated by his teacher. 'Joe Hawksmoor, sir, was her brother-in-law. He was lost in a gale off the Great Barrier Reef in 'seventy-two. Giles, his brother – the husband of our Mrs Hawksmoor – also came to a sticky end when his car plunged over a cliff in Cornwall shortly before their kid was born.

Cushman cocked an eyebrow. 'Accident?'

'It could have been suicide, but for a total lack of motive, sir. That guy had everything: money, looks, a beautiful and happily pregnant wife – it's all in the records. It was decided that he drove too near the cliff edge and fumbled the brake.'

'Any insurance?'

'Quarter of a million.'

'And the company paid up with a smile?'

'They had no option, not with a coroner's straight verdict of "Accidental Death".'

'I'll bet they made their own enquiries, though.'

'That they may have done, sir,' said Orville. 'But it
got them nowhere.'

'Mmmm.'

It had to be faced, sooner or later: the opening of the
fourth door.

Kate had no need to ask herself why she found it
necessary, instead, to clean up the working end of the
studio: shifting an accumulated stack of paintings to the
storeroom, burning an unsavoury pile of dirty paint
rags in the fireplace; ending her task with scarcely any
sense of achievement and the feeling that she had
cheated herself.

At about eleven o'clock, having taken an un-
accustomed drink, and having sat brooding over the
picture of the oval room, she suddenly rose and started
applying paint with frenzied, stabbing strokes of the
palette knife . . .

*We returned to London three months after Pussy was born.
Nannie had wanted us to remain in Goudley, it was better for
the babe, she advised me; but there was a certain selfishness in
my motives for going back to the studio flat: in the first place, I
dearly wanted to see Pussy in the surroundings where her father
and I had spent the greater part of our idyllic time together; add
to which, I had the notion, sooner or later, of returning to some
semblance of the life I had lived before Giles's death. I had a
longing to get back to my studio and paint again – a thing that
I found quite impossible in Goudley, where I contented myself by
making some drawings and studies of Pussy in her cot in the
garden, and of the lush landscape which could be seen from the
staircase window. (I always paint from drawings or from the*

imagination, never from life. My professor at the Royal College believed in the dictum of Renoir and had influenced me to do the same. When asked why he did not paint out of doors, directly from nature, Renoir is said to have replied: 'La peinture ce n'est pas le sport.')

I myself drove the Rolls back to town, with Nannie sitting in the back with Pussy cradled in her arms. I remember that we stopped in a quiet lay-by for Nannie to give my darling some prepared milk-food that we had brought along (it was one of my great regrets that I had been unable to feed Pussy myself), and arrived at the studio flat, which had been thoroughly cleaned out and repainted by a domestic service agency (apart from Giles's study, which I could not bear to have touched) in honour of the new little inhabitant. I myself had designed the colour scheme and furnishings of the nursery; had sent the drawings to a very smart and expensive firm of Mayfair interior decorators, and was longing to see the result.

We let ourselves in. Nannie cried to see the place again, where her adored Master Giles had lived. I cried a little to see the nursery, which was just as I had imagined it, exactly how I had planned it during my long hours of waiting in the sunlit garden back in Goudley. We put Pussy to bed in the fairy-tale cot that, by a near miracle, the interior decorators had managed to match up with my drawing, and went to have a cup of tea.

I threw myself into work the following morning. In the months that followed, I made some of the best paintings of my life so far. My theme was 'Mother and Child', the settings were the Kent countryside round the cottage at Goudley. The central figures were comprised of innumerable variations upon my own appearance – and of Pussy. She I always painted as herself.

Mr Grosse of Morwood, Banks & Grosse wrote and telephoned many times, pressing me to allow him to arrange a one-man exhibition – and could he call round to see the work I had in progress? For reasons I could not then understand, and am only dimly beginning to comprehend now, I stalled and said that I was not yet ready for another show: the line of work I was following had led me into a blind alley, I was destroying more than I was keeping, my principal model had taken off for a holiday – a tissue of the first fabrications that came into my head. Mr Grosse was very patient. He was very happy to wait, he assured me. And he was quite certain that the new work would cause just as much an éclat as my first exhibition.

Gazing at my picture of mother and child, lined up against the long wall of the studio, I could dispassionately agree with the gallery owner's prediction. They were good, really good. And as varied, one from the other, as the movements of a well-constructed symphony. Yet with the main theme persisting: the bond of love that joins mother with child. But they were not for Mr Grosse and the public. They were mine. And Pussy's.

It was in the winter of Pussy's first year that poor Nannie had her first heart attack. It was slight, but, as the doctor informed me, significant. No more stairs for the old lady. No more than the very lightest of work.

Nannie wept when I told her that she must go back to Goudley and a second retirement. She had a younger sister in Leeds, newly-widowed, who was happy to go down to Goudley and join her there. We met her in at King's Cross Station, Pussy, Nannie and I. I was somewhat dismayed to see that the term 'younger sister', as applied to Mrs Fox, was merely a technicality; she looked even more frail and unsteady than poor Nannie. But she won my heart for the way she reacted to Pussy:

insisting on nursing her all the way down to Goudley, calling her 'my little lovey', 'my pet, my Pussy'. I decided that, like her sister, Mrs Fox was a veritable fount of outgoing love.

I left the two old dears to their new life together, promising to bring Pussy to visit them often. In response to Nannie's repeated requests, I also agreed to get a daily woman in to do the housework. Not one of those young flibbertigibbets from the agencies, she enjoined me; that sort were of no use to a working mother; what I needed was a decent, respectable married woman of mature years. I promised to obey her to the letter.

Far from restricting my life, I found to my surprise that Nannie's departure was a blessing in disguise; and it was only then that I realized that I had been, since Pussy's birth, as much nurse to an ailing old lady as to my own child. In fulfilment of my promise, I got a daily woman to do the cleaning, but was quite firm about coping with Pussy myself.

Mrs Holdheim, my 'daily', speedily proved herself to be one of that legendary, rare breed known as 'a treasure'; and when I realized this fact, I unbent slightly and allowed her to baby-sit for me – a circumstance which permitted me to take up, in a very limited sort of way, the 'do-goodery' that had caused Giles so much mild amusement. This I did under the ægis of Lady Coxborough, a rich Chelsea widow who ran the Circle of Ladies for Help, a title of a risible ambiguity which was entirely lost on her ladyship. In fact, the Circle amounted to a dozen or so women of the district, all of them married and pretty well-off, with leisure and boredom on their hands, who were happy for an excuse to get out and do something. We undoubtedly wasted a very great deal of time – our own and other people's – but I like to think that all those rolls we buttered, all those indigent pensioners whom we visited in seedy bed-sits, made some small mark against the supreme indifference of the materialistic world. I certainly found the work – some of the work – very rewarding; and it provided a valuable change of pace from the intensive creativity of painting pictures.

Colin and Cynthia Brierley, when they came, were in turn dismissive and patronizing of Pussy. Colin, who no doubt saw in the two of us his last departed hope of recouping his fortunes (I gathered that he had lost his job in the City and was trying to move into property speculation), opined that she was 'a pretty kid'. His spouse took me aside, said that she had quite fallen in love with the little darling, who was the living image of dear Giles. And could I lend her twenty pounds without letting on to Colin? I gave the money to her without demur, never expecting to see it again – an expectation which proved to be correct.

There is a photo of Pussy and me, taken near the Zoo. Hand in hand, both with ice-cream cones. It was snapped by one of those street photographers whose seedy appearance and spaniel-eyed importuning renders a soft touch like myself quite incapable of offering refusal. Unexpectedly, the photo turned out to be quite interesting, with a fortuitous juxtaposition of Pussy's bobble-hatted little head with the line of bare, winter trees in the background. I used it as the starting-point of yet another painting in my Mother and Child cycle, and with some difficulty resisted the temptation – pace Hockney – to include some lettering in the composition, to illuminate a fragment of dialogue that passed between us on that occasion:

MUMMY: What do you like best of all, darling –
the lions, the tigers, the elephants?

PUSSY: I like the naminals.

With Pussy a very advanced three-year-old, there came the first stirrings of a change in my life. The wound of Giles's loss had healed cleanly, the painting was going well (the Mother and Child series was all but complete), and I knew a curious restlessness that, in my case, usually betokens a yearning to move on to fresh woods and pastures new.

Nannie had died two years previously, and her sister very soon after. A letter from the Hawksmoor family solicitor advised me to sell the Goudley cottage on a 'very buoyant market'; but I decided to move in there permanently. There was no great hurry; first I must complete the Mother and Child paintings, get rid of the studio flat, get rid of the Rolls for something smaller and more practical.

The time had come, for Pussy's sake, to finish my period of mourning. A few tentative steps beyond the sheltered haven of a quiet Chelsea backwater was a tremendously exciting – if slightly alarming – prospect. A prospect that called for some small rejoicing.

I decided to give a party. One of modest dimensions: half a dozen or so people: the partners from Giles's firm and their wives, one of his old school friends and wife. I was not tempted to ask Zoë Chalmers – not that I had her address. And I asked Mr Grosse, adding a note at the corner of the card: Have some pictures to show you.

The day that I sent off the invitations, I started a full-length portrait of my darling Pussy. By the day of the party, it was finished save for a few details of costume; I had decided to leave the background an impressionistic blur.

Shortly after seven-thirty, when I had put Pussy to bed – a nightly ritual of unchanging delight – the first of my guests arrived: one of the partners and his wife. I was a bit put out to discover, after I had enquired about the health of their children, that the lady was a new incumbent; he had divorced and re-

married since the disastrous 'Pre-Coming-out Party'. I had not noticed the change, though she was younger and prettier than his first – as is frequently the case. They probed politely about my life since we had last met, contriving to avoid any mention of Giles. Since I am the recipient of a very considerable quarterly cheque from the firm, I felt it only decent to ask how were things at Lloyds? He was well into a long-winded discourse upon worldwide marine insurance when the rest of my guests arrived more or less en bloc, Mr Grosse bringing up the rear. I made introductions, saw them all fixed up with a drink, then took Mr Grosse aside.

'The pictures . . .'

'You are going to show them to me?' He was an avuncular little man: a Polish Jew who had settled in England after the war, changed his name, entered a son for Eton, and become more English than the English.

'Yes. Now – if you want to see them right away.' I knew in the instant why I had given the party: for no other reason but to show Mr Grosse the Mother and Child cycle.

'Of course, of course!' he responded enthusiastically.

I had laid them out – all fifteen canvases – round the walls of my bedroom. The blinds were drawn against the evening sunlight. Leaving him standing in the middle of the room, I went over and pulled back the blinds, wondering what effect my little piece of stage-managing would have upon the gallery owner. I had quite a while to wait.

He peered round the room, over the top of his half-moon glasses. Then back to the beginning of the line that started by the door; the first in the series: it showed me with Pussy at my breast, with a background of sunflowers, slightly stylized, my foreshortened arm in the foreground leading the eye straight to the exquisite round volumes of the baby's head.

He made no comment; but passed on to the next picture. This he gave scant attention; it was a full-length recumbent of me holding Pussy above my head and laughing up at her. A bit woman's magaziney. I had had my doubts about it, and didn't blame Mr Grosse for dismissing it so readily.

But why did he make no comment, I asked myself, upon the monumental masses of the huge nude – an exaggerated version of myself, myself as Earth-Mother, with the baby in her arms. He gave it five minutes' silent attention, then moved on. Nor did he utter a word till he had made a complete circuit of the room and examined all fifteen pictures.

The silence that followed could have been cut with a knife. Dry-throated, with the tears already starting, I stood in misery, already assembling a comment to break the unbearable tension. So he thought the cycle was worthless? He should know: no art connoisseur, but a hard-headed businessman. I had always liked him for that; heaven preserve an artist from æsthetic picture-dealers who have learned all the jargon from the so-called experts in the intellectual weeklies.

Only – put me out of my misery, Mr Grosse. Tell me that they're a load of mawkish sentiment; that the will of the artist, which should concern itself with plastic values, had been over-laid with the cloying sentimentality of fond motherhood. Or, to put it in your terms, the damn things won't sell because we are not into Chocolate-Box this year.

'Mr Grosse . . .' *I began.*

He turned to face me; spread his hands, hunched his shoulders.

'*What to say, my dear Kate?*'
And I saw that he was crying.

I am trying to pin myself down to the remembrance of the
moment when that evening, which could have been the joyful
turning-point after three years of widowhood and striving,
changed into a nightmare of no awakening; but my mind
constantly returns to the wonder of the moment when it all
might have remained a thing of joy, when Mr Grosse told me
that I had surely fulfilled my tremendous promise, that – in his
words – I had created, by an act of love and a sustained
application of my art, a body of work that would outlive me.

The transition from joy to horror was mundane, not to say
banal, in its mechanics. It was simply a matter of preparing a
bowl of mayonnaise to go with the cold salmon.

'I am shamefully neglecting my other guests, Mr Grosse,' I
told him. 'Would you like to go and get yourself a drink while I
dash into the kitchen and whip up some mayonnaise. Everyone
must be starving.'

'I would much prefer to help you, Kate,' he replied. 'If there
is anything I can do.'

'We'll see,' I said.

My kitchen is next to the studio, where the guests were
gathered. There is a serving surface, and a hatchway opening
into the studio. We heard the murmur of conversation coming
through the closed hatch as we entered the kitchen.

'If you could open a couple of bottles of Chablis, please, Mr
Grosse,' I said. 'They're in the fridge.'

(God – it was as banal as that!)

'Certainly, my dear Kate.'

The adding of oil and vinegar to seasoned egg yolks, while

stirring all the while, not being conducive to higher thoughts on Art, and Mr Grosse being similarly absorbed in the mechanics of drawing bottle corks, we did not resume the conversation we had been having in the other room. But the bumble-bumble of chatter from the studio continued to enter through the hatchway; circulating somewhere on the edge of my consciousness, impersonal as the humming of bees.

Then I heard mention of my dead husband's name, and paused in my stirring.

'Of course, old Giles played the complete cad with the Zoë Chalmers woman.'

The whisk slipped from my hand and I forgot all else.

'Did Kate ever find out, you know, before he was killed?'

'Good lord, no! You know Giles. You should, you were at school with him. Never let his right hand know what his left was doing. And Zoë wasn't likely to make any fuss, considering that Giles settled ten thousand a year on her.'

'Did he, now?'

'Took me into his confidence, he did. We fixed it through the firm's solicitors . . .'

My trembling hand half-overturned the basin. It would have fallen to the floor but for the intervention of Mr Grosse's hand. I met his eyes: dark, Semitic, full of all the agony and compassion of his race.

'The mayonnaise has turned,' I murmured. 'I'll try again.'

'It doesn't matter, Kate,' he whispered. 'Not now.'

'It matters to me?' I breathed, closing my eyes.

His hand upon my shoulder, he said: 'Not now that you have survived and brought up his child so far. Not now that you have fulfilled your great promise. The dead are dead. Those people in there – they are nothing.'

Numbly, I watched him strip off his jacket, roll up his sleeves, prepare a new lot of mayonnaise in the classic manner, and with infinitely more expertise than I have ever possessed. And all the time, my mind screamed out to me: You have been living a lie – the man whose memory you have cherished, whose child you bore, was cheating you right up to the moment of his death. 'Never let his right hand know what the left was doing' – 'Ten thousand a year.'

Ten thousand a year – for what?

A lot of money, surely, for even a rich man to settle upon his mistress. And for life.

Unless . . .

'Voilà – the mayonnaise!' exclaimed Mr Grosse, presenting it to my view.

'Excellent,' I heard myself say.

'Back to your guests,' he said. 'It will not be long. Two hours at the most. You will make polite conversation, from which I shall presently save you by declaring that we must not keep darling Kate up too late because she has work to do tomorrow. We will all depart. You will cry a little. And then you will remember to count your blessings. You will go into your bedroom and regard the pictures which you have created through love and great artistry. Maybe then – yes, I think this is certain – you will tiptoe into the room where your child is sleeping. And you will . . .'

'Mr Grosse . . .' I laid a hand on his arm.

'That is how it will be, eh?'

I kissed his cheek. 'You are a true friend. Without you, I don't think I should get through this evening.'

'But you will get through it.'

I nodded. 'Yes.'

'And it will all be as I have told you.'

I closed my eyes; nodded.

Your advice, your support, is all sound, dear Mr Grosse. For many – for almost anyone – it would suffice.

But not for me . . .

The fourth door was wide open. Kate Hawksmoor had filled the rectangular space with a variant of that painting in the Mother and Child cycle which showed herself as monumental Earth-Mother, nude and bearing in triumph the fruit of her womb. But there was a difference. Instead of Kate Hawksmoor, the pose was taken by the egregious blonde Zoë Chalmers, she of the crisp hair that could be tamed by a running through of the fingers, whose wild-rose and tawny complexion put one so in mind of sunshine and golden youth.

In her arms, she carried a nude child. A boy-child. The image of the dead Giles Hawksmoor.

CHAPTER VII

'INSPECTOR ORVILLE for you, sir.'

'Put him through.'

'You're through, Inspector.'

'Well, Mark?'

'Sir, I've been on to Dr Manners. In fact, I've been round to see him. He squashes the concussion angle flat.'

'Does he, now?'

'Says he dismissed the idea of concussion when he first examined Mrs Hawksmoor on Thursday, and again when he saw her yesterday morning. However, to be on the safe side, he gave her a note to take to hospital for a check-up. She never went to the hospital.'

'Is that significant?'

'Maybe. Anyhow, Manners thinks it's all of a piece with her present irrational behaviour. Seems that she acted very strangely when he was round there yesterday.'

'Strangely – in what way?'

'Concerning the child. When Manners mentioned the child in passing – asked if she was safe and sound – Mrs Hawksmoor nearly hit the ceiling. Accused him of spying on her, and a lot more.'

'How much more, Mark?'

'It was then that the doctor clammed up on me, sir. Said that his professional ethic wouldn't allow him to divulge any more. I pointed out that the Hippocratic Oath didn't extend to the concealment of crime. And that's when *he* hit the ceiling. Said he had not implied crime, only irrational behaviour. There was no concussion in Mrs Hawksmoor's case, he told me. Her problem was purely psychological in his opinion. "Temporary amnesia resulting from unbearable stress" – those were his very words. Further than that he wouldn't go.'

'You mention crime, Mark. Do you think a crime has been committed?'

'Wait till you hear the rest, sir.'

'I'm listening.'

'On a purely routine check, one of our fellows went round to the dealers who supplied the Hawksmoors with the Rolls four years ago, and who've serviced it and kept the log-book up to date ever since. Seems that the car was in for its thirty-six thousand-mile attention only last week and was returned to Mrs Hawksmoor on Tuesday. You'll remember that it was in the early hours of Thursday morning that she was found wandering.'

'So?'

'According to the service records, the Rolls's mile-ometer was almost spot on thirty-six thousand when it was delivered back to Mrs Hawksmoor on Tuesday afternoon late. Between then and when a patrol car found it abandoned some thirty hours later, that car had clocked up another five hundred and fifty-odd miles.'

'The devil it had! Why that's – that's damn nearly to Scotland and back.'

'Or deep Cornwall and back.'

'Why do you say that, Mark?'

'Sir, she went to Cornwall.'

'Let's hear it, Mark.'

'She left the flat and drove away at nine-thirty on Wednesday morning, sir. Now, we're not dealing with a district where folks peer out from behind lace curtains to watch their neighbours' comings and goings. Add to that, the Hawksmoor place has its own private drive that's shrouded with high yew hedges. You could run a whorehouse there for twenty years and never a word of complaint from the folks next door. But, apart from the postman, there's one regular visitor to the Hawksmoor establishment who occasionally sees a thing or two.'

'The milkman.'

'Right. I spoke to him just now at his depot. It was while he was delivering the customary three pints to the Hawksmoors that Mrs H. drove off past him in the Rolls without so much as a glance.'

'With the child?'

'He didn't notice the child, but a three-year-old in the back seat of a big Rolls would scarcely be visible to the casual onlooker as it speeded past.'

' "Speeded," you say?'

'I quote the milkman: "Going like the clappers, and nearly clouted the gatepost on the way out." He heard her take the first corner on screaming tyres.'

'On the way to Cornwall, you say.'

'Right. The speeding didn't do her much good, though. Anyone who's tried to drive to Cornwall at the height of the summer season could have told her she'd come unstuck where the trunk road finishes short of Okehampton and you meet up with the queue of traffic stretching back from the car park at Land's End. Mrs Hawksmoor didn't reach Helston till nearly dusk. We know this because the officers in a patrol car at a roundabout outside Helston sighted a Rolls entering the roundabout in a very dodgy sort of way: a bit too fast, nipping in front of a guy who was already on the circuit – you know the kind of thing: not enough to warrant picking up the driver for a caution, but enough to stick in the mind. They noted down the registration number, also that there was a woman driver.'

'How did this very insignificant piece of information find its way back to us?'

'It didn't, sir. Playing a hunch, I came round here to the local nick and telexed details of the Rolls to every police headquarters operating along the three hundred-odd radius of London, and got lucky. As soon as I had the Helston report, I knew I was on to something.'

'Which was . . .?'

'The cliff – that cliff down which Mrs Hawksmoor's husband took a fatal nose-dive in his car three years ago, sir – is less than ten miles' drive from Helston.'

A long pause . . .

'Are you still there, sir? What now? Do we move in on Mrs Hawksmoor and put the question to her: "What have you done with your child?" – in as many words.'

'You're at the local nick, you say?'

'Yes, sir.'

'I'll be right round. Alert the Cornish people for a missing child. Ask them to search the site of the cliff.'

'And Mrs Hawksmoor?'

'Mmm. Let's see – what time is it? Twelve-fifteen. I think we'll lay off her till we get an answer back from Cornwall one way or the other. After all, Mark, she won't be going anywhere we don't know about today, will she?'

She would finish the picture today. The last – and most awful – remembrance of all lay behind the fifth door, and had to be faced. Meanwhile, it was a blessed respite from her labours merely to lie on the sofa, with the picture – which she now hated – standing beyond the range of her vision; to enjoy the cool air that gently rustled the curtains of the open windows looking out on to the drive; to shut the mind against all assaults of remembrance; merely to be in a state of total unfeeling . . .

What was that?

Someone coming up the drive.

Kate uncoiled herself from her cushioned ease and ran, barefoot, to the window.

It was Jock Carter – as she might have known. She relaxed. The man from the Antipodes had kept his promise of a tryst with his 'new baby', as he had called the Rolls. Clad in a T-shirt and slacks, his blue-black hair tousled like a boy's, he was slowly pacing round the car, arms akimbo, lips pursed in a soundless whistle; and now he paused in front of the bonnet and was running his hand along the dent she had made, as if, by an effort of will and love, he could heal the injured metal.

On an impulse, Kate ran to fetch her handbag. He looked up and met her gaze, pulling aside the curtain, she leaned out of the open window.

'Hi, Kate. Good day to you,' he called out.

'Hello.'

'Getting better acquainted with my new baby – as you see.'

'Yes, I've been watching you. I wonder – if you'd like to go for a drive in her.'

'Would I not? Sure you trust me to bring her back? Me with my joke cheque.'

For answer, she tossed the key. It sailed across the open space between them, a winking scrap of silvery metal in the sun.

One hand on high, he caught it effortlessly.

'Thanks, Kate. You've made an old man very happy. I'll bring it back in – shall we say an hour?'

'Take as long as you like,' she replied, and watched him give a thumbs-up sign and climb into the driving seat. The engine purred to life. She turned back to regard the sunlit studio interior – and the shadowed part in the far corner, where she had wheeled the big easel on its castors, away from the range of her vision. The four open doors stood out brightly against the sombre hues of the oval-shaped room in the picture: sunlight and colour contrasting with shadowed drabness. The fifth door awaiting to be opened.

Crossing to the easel, she wheeled it over towards the window, into a patch of light.

Full light, in which to drag out the last of the secrets from her clouded mind.

Kate poured herself a stiff gin – she who had never found need of either drink or drugs to heighten her perception; took a deep swig of the spirit; picked up palette and brushes, and prepared to lift the last veil . . .

They left the party before midnight, gently shepherded out by Mr Grosse, who lingered at the door for a few moments, kissed my cheek and murmured in my ear:

'Good night, my dear Kate. You have had a few glasses of wine that is good. Now you will sleep. Sleep – and forget. Leave tomorrow to look after itself. Yesterday is dead.'

'Good night, Mr Grosse,' I said.

'Promise me you will do nothing silly.'

'I will do nothing – silly.'

A slamming of car doors mingled with last goodnights. Whirring of starter motors, engines coming to life. Crunch of tyres on the gravel. The sounds fading off into the night.

I was alone – yet not alone.

Back in the studio, looking at the recently occupied seats, the abandoned litter of the evening: cigarette ends, olive stones, glasses rimmed with lipstick and plain, the ghost of an appalling secret that had been bruited around and still hung in the air – for ever defiling the room. I poured myself a tumbler full of gin and drank it down like water; choked and gagged on the neat spirit and nearly threw up; slumped down upon the sofa after pouring another glassful.

Memories – images . . .

Zoë Chalmers in the green cocktail dress she had worn that night of the 'Pre-Coming-out Party'; wanton-eyed, brazen, the huntress of men. Very capable girl. No wonder she set her cap at Giles, who was by far the most attractive man present: rich also, and with a pregnant wife. Available.

It was soon after, was it not, that Giles floated the idea of the branch office down in Plymouth. His idea entirely, for he told me about it, how he had steered it through a stormy board meeting. The other directors had not thought much of travelling down to the West Country, so Giles himself had volunteered to act as liaison between the City office and Plymouth.

Between the fourth month of my pregnancy and the day that the dumpy little plainclothes police lady brought me the news, Giles must have made – how many? – trips and stayed over-night. Did I need to ask with whom?

With Zoë Chalmers – who else? Did she travel with him? Unlikely. Probably they met up in the evening at a hotel. Somewhere large, impersonal, discreet.

My glass was empty. And I had not spilled a drop. Who, I asked myself, is that attractive woman in the pier glass? – the woman in the cocktail dress, with dark hair and a somewhat over-large mouth. Ooops, she's overturned the bottle. Let it drip off the table and into the glass. Clever lady.

He gave her a brat. Why else the ten thousand a year?

While I was carrying Pussy, he gave the bitch a brat. Ten thousand a year for life. And there'll be a love-nest somewhere, that's for sure. Not that I cared, for my hatred was all for him, the man I had loved, who was taken from me, and returned in the form of the child whom I had borne three weeks later. A life transferred, a love that bridged the span of death. Husband and wife. Mother and Child.

*I threw the empty gin bottle at my reflection in the pier glass;
flinched when the mirror cracked into a spider's web; fell.
Part of the broken bottle, the neck and the upper half, rolled
towards my feet. I stooped to pick it up by the neck. Three long
shards of glass stood out like daggers, honed in an instant of
time to the sharpness of surgeons' scalpels.*

*Unsteadily, supporting herself against the wall, the woman
whose reflection had been destroyed in the pier glass, went out
of the studio and up the stairs to the bedroom. The door was
still open.*

*Mother and Child. The theme of a love that had bridged
the span of death. The destroyed woman threw back her head
and laughed.*

'A body of work created by love . . . It will outlive
you.'

'Oh no, it bloody well won't!'

*Then the destroyed woman was cutting, slashing at paint
and canvas.*

*When she had finished, her hair hung about her head in
sweat-soaked rats' tails. The broken bottle in her hand, when
she examined it closely, had shreds of paint-daubed canvas
impaled upon its points and jammed into its interstices, hanging like new-flayed skin. She laughed again; shouted to the
ceiling:*

*'All for you, Giles Hawksmoor! To think it was all done
in memory of you!'*

*I was certainly insane when I reeled out of the bedroom and
made my way to the door at the end of the passage, though,
with the cunning of the insane, I trod lightly so as not to wake*

the sleeping child, fearful all the time that I might already have done so.

The door handle turned smoothly and silently. No sound within. A pink-shaded night-light burned near the foot of the fairy-tale cot with its two tall pillars meeting at the head, all surmounted by a fairy crown. Tiptoeing closer, I could see the angle of a smooth cheek against the pillow, and one small fist clenched at the edge of the patchwork blanket, a lock of flaxen hair – his hair *– curled across her brow.*

Personified in the child, it lay there: the image of a love that I had cherished past death and into a new life. A love that, now, I knew to have been spurned and defiled.

And now it was all over . . .

Kate shuddered, stepped back from the canvas, and, narrowing her eyes, made an appraisal of what she had done so far in the opened fifth door. In so doing, she became aware of the ringing of her front doorbell: a jarring and insistent sound that cut through her concentration and dissolved the images that had come alive in her mind. Nor did it cease; whoever was there was firmly intent upon being received. With a last glance at the still unfinished picture, she laid aside her brush and palette and went to answer it.

'To collect the desk, lady. And the other items. One swivelling office chair, one marquetry table, one corner cupboard of oak, one Persian rug.' The speaker was a large man of bovine appearance clad in workman's overalls and a flat cap. He read the items from a scuffed notebook, ticking them off with a stub of pencil which he had first moistened with his tongue.

Over the bulky line of his shoulder, Kate could see a large van with the legend PARKER'S REMOVALS painted on its steep side. Another individual in long apron – a thin youth in glasses – descended from the cab, stubbed out a cigarette under his foot, stooped and, picking up the butt, tucked it carefully above his ear.

'I – I don't know what you mean,' said Kate. 'There must be some mistake.'

The large man eyed her reflectively, then returned to his notebook.

'Name of Hawksmoor?' he queried.

'Yes,' she breathed.

'Mrs Hawksmoor?'

'Yes, that's right. But what has all this to do with me?'

He sniffed. 'To collect the desk and other items, purchased from Mrs K. Hawksmoor by The Treasure Chest, Kings Road, and deliver to The Treasure Chest. That's all I know, lady. Them's my orders.'

She became aware that reality was slipping away from her again. Yet, somewhere far off, she had an image of herself – and surely it must have been a lifetime away – in an outgoing and optimistic frame of mind; a time when she had decided to get rid of the Rolls, sell the contents of the flat, starting with the most poignantly evocative of the lot: the furnishings of Giles's study, his old-fashioned roll-top desk, chair, cupboard. And, surely, someone had come: a prim, small man with a bald head and thick glasses, who had given her a cheque and had informed her that the items

would be collected later in the week. Had it happened
so recently? Horrifying that she should have forgotten!

'Yes, of course,' she said. 'It had – slipped my mind.
Will you come in?'

He sniffed again, cocked his eyes to the rear. 'Come
on, Darren!' he called. 'We've got the right place.'

The two of them trooped after her, their big boots
resounding loudly on the parquet flooring of the
studio; through the archway that led to Giles's study,
up the three steps. Inside, the open desk and all *his*
papers littering the blotter, the untouched detritus of
his life.

'I'm afraid it's all in rather a mess,' said Kate
weakly. 'My late husband had this room and I've never
got round to clearing it up.'

The large man unbent considerably. His moist,
fleshy lips assumed a sketchy smile. 'Not to worry,
lady,' he said. 'We'll empty the drawers and pigeonholes and pile everything up against the wall.'

'Thank you,' said Kate, and, searching her mind for
some way to make her exit: 'Er, would you like a cup
of tea?'

'That'll be very acceptable, lady,' said the large man.

'Three lumps of sugar, missus,' said the youth
Darren.

They were pulling out the drawers of the desk when
she left. In the kitchen, waiting for the kettle to boil, her
mind nagged her about the unfinished picture, the
interruption in the last unveiling of her secret: the true
account of her love and motherhood; the history of
betrayal, death, and the renouncing of love.

In the first door: Giles. A man who had loved her
according to his lights. A man fatally flawed by having
been raised in the great shadow of an elder brother
whom he had both idolized and envied; in whose footsteps he had vainly tried to tread. It explained so much:
to be worthy of Joe's memory, he had risked his neck at
point-to-point, driven fast cars, tried to fly aeroplanes.
In Joe's memory, he had carried to his grave the shotgun pellet that his brother had fired into his breast.
And it had all been in vain; in trying to find his own
identity through the image of his idol, he had lost himself. Having lost himself, he had cast about for re-
assurance from whatever quarter that offered. From
Kate Gregg. From Zoë Chalmers. And how many
others?

She supposed that it must have been more than pre-
natal tension that had led her to accuse him of carrying-
on with Zoë during the party. How smoothly he had
been able to quench her fears. And it was more than
likely that their affair had been going on for some time
by then, and that the old school-friend who had
brought Zoë to the party had been in the know . . .

Her dark reverie was interrupted by the whistling of
the kettle. She made the tea, emptied a few dry
biscuits on to a plate; put teapot, milk jug, sugar bowl,
cups, on to a tray and carried it to the study.

All that mattered, now, was to get the men off the
premises as soon as possible – together with what they
had come to fetch (what poignancy, now, did the detritus of her faithless husband's life evoke?).

The roll-top desk had been carried out into the

middle of the room, together with the office chai , the marquetry table, the oak cupboard which had been taken down from the wall, the rolled-up Persian rug. And the contents of the drawers and pigeonholes were neatly stacked against the wall.

Darren peered at her short-sightedly. 'Tea up,' he said.

The large man beamed. 'A whole pot o' tea!' he exclaimed. 'You're doing us real proud, lady.' He took the tray from her and laid it in the middle of the marquetry table. 'Will you be Mother and pour, Darren, or should I?' he asked.

Kate, in the act of turning to go, was instantly stricken with a curious sense of something having admitted itself to a corner of her mind; so that she paused, searching for what it might have been, and was still standing, irresolute, with her back to the two men, when the youth Darren said:

'Hey, we've forgotten the note, Jack.'

'So we have, so we have. Here we are, lady. Must be yours.'

It was a complete act of *déja vu*. She knew upon the instant what he held in his hand; knew what it was that her eye had encompassed and printed upon her retina in the brief instant of time when she had glanced at the marquetry table. She turned – and it was so.

'Found it behind the desk, lady,' said the man Jack. 'Could've been lying there for quite a while, p'raps.'

She took it from him. It was an envelope of the elongated shape that Giles Hawksmoor preferred: an expensive piece of stationery in thick bond, an example of one of his minor extravagances which had been so much at odds with his small economies like, for instance, saving old pieces of string and wrapping paper. Written across the face of it, in Giles's dashing Italic script, was the single word that had insinuated itself upon her mind a few moments earlier:

Darling

'Yes, it – it's been there quite a while,' she whispered.

CHAPTER VIII

ALONE AGAIN in the flat, the men having gone, it became important to think the thing through; to peel away the layers of time that obfuscated memory, to relive the summer's morning three years ago, the morning that Giles had left the flat for the last time, to keep his tryst with death below a Cornish cliff; which having been done, she might dare to open the envelope and discover what had been his final message to her, a message that, due to some mischance – a draught of air from the open window? – had become a message from beyond the grave.

Think, girl. Think . . .

The envelope, unopened and propped up against a pot containing paint brushes, stood before her, beckoning her.

How had Giles been on that last evening before his departure? Gentle and considerate, as ever – of that she had no doubt. The trouble was that she had no particular recollection. Heavily pregnant and totally self-absorbed and self-regarding, she had been in no condition to notice any but the most gross changes of mood and manner in others. Even in Giles, whom she had loved so completely.

She *must* remember. His manner on that evening might give a clue to the contents of the envelope. (She had dismissed the notion that the message might be of a petty and trivial nature; instinctively, she knew it to be something of significance, though she had nothing but intuition to tell her so.) The trouble was that, at that stage of her pregnancy, she had suffered a lot of tiredness, and Giles had moved into the spare room, leaving her alone in their great double bed. On that night, as on many others preceding it, there could have been no endearments other than a goodnight kiss, and his usual 'Sleep well, darling'.

No clue to be found there; nor in the events of the following morning, for she had slept late, as had become her habit at that stage. Giles had got up, made his own coffee and toast, departed in his old Aston-Martin (starting the engine as quietly as possible and taking it slowly out of the drive so as not to awaken her), leaving the note propped up on the top of his desk where she would see it immediately on entering. (He knew well that she had taken to using his suavely-padded office chair because she found it rested her back muscles – they had joked about it often.)

If recollection provided no answer, then she must rely on reasoning. There were not many options. Triviality was out. There remained only two possibilities, and she faced the first one quite squarely. There had been talk at the inquest – she had read it in the back numbers of newspapers long afterwards – about the possibility of Giles having committed suicide.

Was the thing that beckoned her from the painting table his suicide note? Had his affair with Zoë escalated to a crisis where he had felt obliged to take his own life? The inquest coroner, taking all things into account, had dismissed the possibility of suicide. On far, far better evidence – knowing Giles's heartfelt, almost savage, love of life – so did she.

There remained only one other option, and she shrank from the contemplation of it; the near-certainty in her mind that the envelope did, indeed, contain the thing she most dreaded had prevented her from ripping it open immediately; instead, she had desperately sought around for another possibility. No such possibility existed.

Triviality out. Suicide out. The letter was to tell her that he was leaving her for Zoë Chalmers, the woman upon whom he had settled a very large sum of money, the woman who was almost certainly the mother of his . . .

With a cry of despair, Kate leapt forward and snatched up the envelope; ripped it open with such violence as to tear in half the sheet of writing paper that lay within, so that she was constrained to fit it together in order to decipher the message that entered upon her consciousness; slowly at first, like the hesitant beginning of a glorious theme in music, then mounting to a crescendo of realization, of sudden splendour, and a wonder beyond all imagining.

Kate, my darling,

Here is how it is: I have made a slight hash of my life; today I am going to un-hash it. Useless for me to try and explain. That I may do on Thursday, when I get home. Or maybe the explanations will have to wait till the Thursday

after. Or maybe till eternity. But, believe me, I love you.
And I shall be home, and loving you still.

                    Yours, my darling Kate,

                                    G.

Trembling, she slipped to her knees beside the chair, buried her face in her hands.

'I was wrong,' she whispered through her tears. 'I have been wrong all this time. He loved me, after all. And he was on his way to break with her.'

And then: 'Oh, Pussy – what a dreadful, dreadful waste!'

The campers and caravanners at Trewinn Farm, after having suffered another night of torrential rain followed by a day of overcast, had rejoiced at the promising new morn. The owner of the site, not a Cornishman himself, but a Yorkshireman from Huddersfield, a tall and rangy man with Cornish attitudes inculcated after twenty-five years' residence in the Duchy, opined to his wife that, considering the sun was not enough to lure down to the beach, three miles distant, 't'bloody 'Immets' (which is the Cornish word for tourists as also for ants. The scarcely less laudatory term in adjacent Devon is 'Grockles') it was very obliging of the local police to put on a show for them on the clifftop and get the surly, complaining mob off the camp site.

And so it was. Half a hundred bored and sunkissed holidaymakers from the Midlands and the Metropolis, from Scotland and the Eastern Counties; grey-rinsed, paunched, sandalled, pert and bra-less, corseted and rheumy-eyed; old, young and middling, stood in a wide semi-circle near the cliff edge, watching a group of local CID men and uniformed police go about their arcane and fascinating business.

'That feller with the inch-tape, he's measuring them car tracks.'

'T'other, he's takin' a sample o' the soil.'

'Wayne, stop pickin' your nose and watch. It's very educational.'

'Look, here comes the big man. He must be an inspector at least.'

A middle-aged man in civilian clothes was saluted as he got out of a patrol car. He nodded acknowledgement.

'How's it going?'

'There was a car here all right, sir. Thanks to the Immets, the footprints are a hotch-potch, nothing for us there, but the tyre tracks are as clear as handwriting. We're going to take a cast right now. And that isn't all . . .'

They walked in a body to the cliff edge. The speaker pointed.

'It was dragged the last few yards. See it, sir?'

'Box of some kind.'

'Suitcase or hamper.'

They looked down. The tide was out, revealing a perilously narrow strip of shingle at the base of the sheer cliff, over which the incoming waves, as if grudging the vestige of their domain briefly given over to the outer world, constantly lapped. There were three men in wading boots down there, all carrying metal-detectors, which they swung from side to side over the glistening shale, backwards and forwards, slowly pacing to and fro along the cliff bottom.

'It puts me in mind,' said one of the watchers, 'of the time we had that feller in the car down there. Three years ago, it was.'

'I mind the trouble we had to get the car up,' said another. 'Had to fetch a fifteen-ton crane all the way fro Truro.'

There was a ripple of nervous laughter from the watchers, as a larger wave than most swept, knee-high, upon the men below, causing them to reel back against the stark granite. One of them dropped his instrument.

'I'll be getting back,' said the senior officer. 'Call me if they come across anything. I'll ring London and tell them about the tracks.'

'Very good, sir.' The others saluted.

Hardly had the patrol car vanished down the rutted lane – and the campers, bored with the proceedings, were beginning to drift back to their tents and caravans – when one of the searchers at the cliff bottom paused in his sweeping to and fro, knelt in the shingle, ferreted around for a moment or two, and dug up something which he held on high to show the officers above.

'He's got something. Lower a line for it.'

'She's gone, sir – she's taken the Rolls and gone!'

'What are you telling me, Mark? Are you telling me that you didn't order a car round to watch Mrs Hawksmoor's place the instant you put down the phone from ringing me?'

'That I did, sir,' said Orville. 'And they were round there in good time, considering that they ran head-on into a smash-and-grab in Kensington High Street on the way. They reported in just now. The car's gone. She's blown. But she won't be hard to find. Not in a car like that. Not in a car like that with a dented front.'

'There's a call out for her?'

'Done, sir. Every available car in the Metropolitan area. She can't stay at large for more than another quarter of an hour.'

'What about the smash-and-grab in Kensington High Street?'

'The villains were new boys and dead amateurs. Ran headlong into a bus when they tried to make a getaway. One of them actually burst into tears when the lads in the patrol car arrested him. A mere kid.'

Cushman had set up what amounted to a temporary command post in the local police station: a spare office with a desk and telephone. They had provided him with a mug of tea and had sent out for some sandwiches. It was half past one.

'Want some tea?' he demanded of his subordinate.

'Thanks, no. I've tried the tea at this nick.' Orville pulled a face and took from his pocket a typewritten flimsy. 'By the way, sir, I've got some more background on the Hawksmoors and relations. It wasn't difficult, because a file was started with the Giles Hawksmoor death. And there was a cross-reference with the Fraud Squad.'

'Was there, now? Not the dead man, surely – he was gilt-edged.'

'Colin Brierley, the cousin who phoned in the first 999.'

'Tell.'

'For starters, Brierley stands to inherit all of the late Giles Hawksmoor's estate on the demise of Mrs Hawksmoor and the child Priscilla. And his background is, to say the least, somewhat gamey.'

'Oh yes?' Cushman took out his pipe and filled it, conscious of the glance of distaste that his subordinate threw at him.

'Brierley served in the regular army for three years,' said Orville. 'Reached the rank of lieutenant. Resigned his commission following a scandal concerning misappropriation of mess funds. No charges were brought. Out in civvy street, through the good graces of his cousin Giles, who spoke a few words in the right places, we find Brierley walking into a sinecure in the City – the sort calling for a bowler hat, a briefcase, and the capacity to stay awake through board meetings. Three months ago, Brierley was fired. Fraud squad inform us that there may be charges brought against him and several of his fellow-directors.'

'A bad 'un,' said Cushman, puffing the while.

'A classic cad,' said Orville. 'What used to be called a regular thoroughgoing bounder. And it isn't finished yet. Out of a job, Brierley starts dabbling in property deals of a very unsavoury kind. His wife doesn't know it, but he's already filed a petition for bankruptcy. The man's in real trouble.'

'Interesting,' said Cushman. 'Might be worth bearing in mind.'

'I thought so, sir,' said his junior, crossing to open the window.

She had read Giles's last note a hundred times; weighing each word and phrase, extracting from it every possible nuance and shade of meaning and implication. From every angle, his intentions remained, to her, as clear as they had been at the first, glorious reading.

When he had left her that morning, it had been with the intention of keeping an assignation with Zoë Chalmers, of breaking with her and of returning home a different man; a man who had severed an illicit bond. That had been his intent. Tragically that intent had been thwarted by – *what*?

By fate?

She remembered the speculations in the newspaper reports of the inquest: the laborious evidence for and against suicide; the grudging acceptance of the fact that, against all probability, Giles had somehow fumbled his brakes on that hazardous cliff edge, so that the car had rolled forward down a gentle slope to the edge.

She took a deep breath and tried again. Take it from Zoë Chalmers's viewpoint. Presume that Zoë had been unaware – as well she might – that her paramour was on his way to break with her; but was keeping a regular weekly assignation. There was she, with an attractive and attentive lover, recipient of a very considerable settlement. Kate tried to remember the woman as she had been on the only occasion they had met: at the disastrous party: the managing, masterful creature who had had everyone running round in circles at the snap of her well-manicured finger. Was she the sort who would allow herself to be tossed aside without putting up a fight? Or to be deprived of her cosy *dot* at what she would doubtless regard as the whim of a stupid, capricious male? No, she would not; she would fight like a wildcat. And, in the process, someone could get hurt.

Killed, even . . .

With a choked cry, Kate rushed across the studio to pick up the telephone directory; riffled through the dog-eared pages; Challis – Challoner – Chalmers, Suzanne – Chalmers Health Foods – She tossed the volume aside and dialled Enquiries. A long pause, followed by a remarkably co-operative girl at the other end of the line. No, there appeared to be no subscriber of that name in the London area. Thank you.

Think! Think . . .

The man who had brought Zoë to the party: the old school-friend, who had almost certainly been in on the act and must surely at one time have been a lover of the accommodating Zoë (and hadn't he got himself married soon after the party?) must know where she lived. But what was his name? Peter something, but Peter what? And he lived in London. She checked the address book, but both she and Giles had always been careless about keeping it up to date. It offered no clues. Surely, there had to be some way of pin-pointing this man, who had

known Giles ever since they were at School together.
School!

The notion sent her running into Giles's study:
empty now, save for the piles of papers, books, stationery, elastic bands, pencils, bits and bobs, that Jack
and Darren had dutifully stacked against the wall. She
fell to her knees by the books; upset the piles in uncaring abandon till she found what she sought: a dozen
or so copies of his, Giles's, old school magazine. She
looked for the dates on the covers. The one she wanted
was surely dated four summers previously. Her heart
leapt to see it, and melted with a sudden anguish – as
Giles's face smiled out from the photograph of the Old
Boys' Cricket XI. How young he looked: blond and
handsome in his white shirt and flannels, the cable-knit
sweater she had made for him herself. And the Old
Boy standing next to him was the man she sought. Her
eye skimmed along the caption: *Hawksmoor, G. L.;
Walker, P. J.*

Peter Walker answered the phone; she knew his voice
immediately because it was – as she remembered –
high-pitched and affected.

'Who is that?'

'Kate Hawksmoor. How are you, Peter?'

'Oh – er, I'm fine, thank you – er, Kate. And yourself?' He sounded embarrassed, as well he might, if her
speculation about him was correct.

'Very well, thank you. Peter, I am ringing to ask a
favour.'

'Name it, please do.'

'I'd like you to give me Zoë Chalmers's address and telephone number.'

She distinctly heard his sharp intake of breath. Meeting her eyes in the mirror opposite, she marvelled to see how calm and resolute she looked.

Presently he said: 'I – I'm afraid I can't be of any help, Kate. I simply don't have it.'

'Oh, but I think you have, Peter,' she countered calmly.

A pause, then: 'Why should you think that?'

'Because Zoë was your mistress before she was Giles's.'

'I see,' he said. 'So that's the way it is. I think this is where I hang up on you, Kate.'

'Hang up on me, and I come straight round to see you, Peter. Is your wife at home?'

'Hold on a moment . . .' She heard the other receiver being laid down upon a table top; his footsteps receded, a door closed; he returned. 'Look here, Kate, I don't know what your game is, but I don't want any trouble.'

'There'll be no trouble – for you – if you simply give me her address and phone number.'

'But, dammit, Kate. Why dredge up the past? Giles is dead . . .'

'Giles is my concern! Your concern is to keep out of trouble! Give me what I want!' She stared unbelievingly at her reflection in the mirror. Was this *really* the nervous, withdrawn Kate Hawksmoor?

A pause, then: 'She gave up her London flat ages ago. Spends all her time at her cottage in Norfolk. The address is Church Gate Cottage, Wingham.'

'And the phone number?'

He gave it to her. She wrote it down beside the address.

'Kate,' he said, 'do I have your promise that you won't be stirring up any old mud?'

'You do not have my promise,' said Kate. 'But none of the mud will hit you – not if I can help it. Thank you, Peter. And goodbye.'

She hung up; dialled another number, heard it ring out for a long time in a surely empty room. How was life, she thought, in Church Gate Cottage, Wingham? It sounded an uncommonly unsuitable address for the egregious Zoë Chalmers. Had the blonde seductress become tame with the years? Did she do good works around the village? Dressed in tweeds and sensible shoes, was she on the roster for cleaning the church altar brasses and arranging the flowers? Was she . . .?

The line crackled. A voice said: 'Wingham two-three-six.'

Her voice!

Kate lowered the receiver.

Beware, Zoë – *for I am coming*!

CHAPTER IX

CUSHMAN HAD SMOKED three pipes. Despite the open window, the narrow office was thick with tobacco fug, for the air was heavy, hot and still, and the tarmac was steaming in the street outside. Cushman was tieless and in shirt sleeves. He wiped his brow with a spotted handkerchief, and thought of the cool shade of his garden in Bromley.

'It's been a damn long quarter of an hour,' he grumbled. 'Two-fifteen, and our Mrs Hawksmoor's still on the loose. And her Rolls.'

Orville hunched his shoulders. 'Unless she's driven that car into cover, she doesn't have a hope in hell,' he said.

A uniformed constable entered, after knocking. 'Telex from Devon and Cornwall Constabulary, sir.' He laid the sheet down on the desk in front of Cushman, who scanned it and whistled.

'What's new, sir?' asked Orville.

'This seems to clinch it, Mark,' replied Cushman. 'They've been very good, the local chaps. Very thorough. The positive impression of a motor-car's tyres, of type and wheelbase that indicate a Rolls, has been found on that clifftop. And they're sending up a plaster cast by dispatch-rider, for comparison. And that's not all. There's the trail of something having been dragged through wet and muddy turf to the cliff edge and shoved over. They suggest a large suitcase.'

'Big enough to hold a body?' suggested Orville.

'Perhaps,' said Cushman. 'They don't say. But they also found something at the bottom of the cliff in low tide. Look . . .' He tossed the sheet to his subordinate, who caught it.

Orville read: ' "A child's bracelet. Silver." That'll be interesting to see, sir. And shouldn't be too difficult to trace.'

'Pity we can't cut corners on that one and trace it immediately,' said Cushman. 'Got any ideas, Mark?'

Orville scratched the side of his nose, was silent for a few moments; then snapped his finger and thumb.

'Harrods!' he exclaimed.

'Mrs Hawksmoor has an account there!' Cushman pointed his pipe, like a pistol, at his subordinate. 'The inventory of the contents of her handbag included a Harrods' credit card. It's worth trying, Mark. Don't use this phone, I want to keep it clear for incoming calls.'

His last instruction was quite unnecessary, for Orville was half-way to the door before it was delivered. He was back ten minutes later, giving his chief the 'thumbs-up' sign.

'Got it?' demanded Cushman.

Orville looked smug. 'According to Harrods' records, a bracelet such as we describe was purchased on September fifteenth of last year by Mrs Hawksmoor.'

'September fifteenth!' From a buff-coloured letter wallet that lay before him, Cushman extracted a birth certificate that had been collected from Somerset

House a short time before by a police dispatch-rider. Orville looked over his shoulder. They both registered the significant fact in unison.

'The child Priscilla was born on September seventeenth, which is two days after her mother bought the gift!'

Orville's long knobbly finger touched the paper. 'Look, the mother's an honourable, sir,' he said. 'It says here: Mother: the Hon. Kate Hawksmoor, née Gregg.'

'Only daughter of the first, late, and only Baron Gregg, who was made an hereditary Labour peer during the Attlee government,' said Cushman. 'There was no male heir to succeed him, so the creation fell dormant.'

'You're well up on the peerage, sir,' said Orville.

'Debrett's *Peerage* and Burke's *Landed Gentry* are my favourite bedside reading, Mark,' said Cushman. 'I am a tremendous snob.'

'Is that so, sir?' said Orville.

'So this is what we have,' said Cushman. Laying a matchbox across the bowl of his pipe, he sucked air briskly. The tobacco sparked like fireworks. 'Mrs Hawksmoor takes off for Cornwall in a hurry on Wednesday morning. That evening, she is sighted near Helston. The Rolls is later parked on the cliff at a spot where her husband met his end three years ago. Indications are that a suitcase or other large container was dragged from the car boot and pushed over the cliff. Mrs Hawksmoor's child's birthday bracelet is found at the foot of the said cliff.'

'The case probably burst open on impact with the water,' supplied Orville. 'Or from the action of the waves smashing it against the cliff face. The body was thrown out, and the bracelet became detached.'

Their eyes met.

'We do not have a body,' murmured Cushman. 'Not yet, we don't.'

'We have a strong presumption,' replied the other. 'What next, sir?'

Cushman consulted his watch. 'Time's passing, and all the patrol cars in the Met seem unable to locate that Rolls. She's gone to earth, Mark. What we do now is move into that flat of hers and see what we can turn up in the way of evidence. Fix a search warrant immediately, will you?'

Orville was already on his way.

Kate changed into jeans and a linen shirt; tied her hair into a navy silk scarf, put on a pair of dark glasses. And regarded the result in a mirror. Portrait of a murderess.

From out of a drawer in a papier-mâché jewel case that she had bought while on honeymoon in Paris, she took a hatpin: a length of tapering steel surmounted by a knob of twisted filigree set with pearls. It had belonged to her mother; she herself had never owned a hat in her life. The needle-sharp point, when she brushed it across the tip of her thumb, seemed to have an energy of its own, seemed eager to leap forward and pierce skin and flesh. It would take hardly any effort, she guessed, to drive it fully home . . .

I am your Nemesis, Zoë. The scales have fallen

from my eyes and I see it all so clearly. They were
wrong three years ago, the police, the insurance people,
the coroner and his court. Not an accident, nor yet
suicide, destroyed Giles Hawksmoor. It was by your
hand.

You made an end to all I loved in the world. And
now you are going to pay, Zoë.

She balled up a handkerchief, stabbed the point of
the bodkin into it for safety's sake, and laid the weapon
in the bottom of her handbag. A minute later, she let
herself out of the front door of the flat and walked
quickly down the drive, turned left towards the
King's Road.

She would have preferred to have made her journey
in the Rolls; that would have had a certain rightness;
but she could not wait for Jock Carter's return, for the
thing she was setting out to do, having once been
decided upon, would not wait. An hour, even half an
hour, of waiting and inaction might blunt her resolve.
She must move now, and move fast.

She went down the quiet, tree-lined roads, her
sandalled feet silent upon the sun-baked flagstones. A
dark and slender woman with a murder weapon concealed in her handbag. An elderly gentleman of military
cut, walking a Pekingese on a lead, raised his straw hat
to her in passing. Behind ornamental railings, an
automatic lawn-sprinkler weaved and turned like a
charmed snake. From far off there came the distant sigh
of the great city's traffic.

The next turning brought her into a deserted mews,
with a line of cars parked along its shady side. Deliber-

ately slowing her step, she changed direction slightly, so as to pass close by the drivers' doors. The first was an open-topped sports of foreign make; the next a sleek limousine; then a family saloon with a crumpled wing. She walked three paces past a red Mini that had a bunch of keys dangling from its ignition lock; paused and looked about her. No one in sight. The driver's door was open, and she slipped into the seat. The engine started briskly.

No one saw her drive the red Mini out of the mews, and she excited not the slightest attention – for why should she? – when she turned right into the King's Road and joined the eastbound flow of mid-afternoon traffic heading for the heart of the city and the main arteries radiating from the heart.

At about the same time as the red Mini was speeding eastwards along the North Circular Road, a pair of police cars nosed into the drive outside her flat. Cushman and Orville were in the back of the lead car. As if in a gesture of delicacy, they distanced themselves from the uniformed officers from the second car, who gained entrance to the establishment by means known not only to the criminal classes.

'Opened up, sir.'

'Come on, Mark,' said Cushman. 'Let's see what Mrs Hawksmoor's left for us.'

They entered, mounted the three steps that led straight into the studio room. Cushman sniffed the air, looked towards the tall easel that stood against the far wall, bearing a canvas shrouded with a sheet.

'That, from what the officer who was here on Thursday tells me, is the kid,' said Orville, pointing to the portrait leaning against the wall. 'That's Priscilla – or Pussy, as Mrs H. called her.' He was already using the past tense.

Cushman scanned the delicate, unformed features in the picture.

'Sad-looking little thing,' he mused.

'And with good reason, I should think,' said Orville harshly. 'What have we got here?' He crossed over to the easel and drew back the concealing sheet. 'Well, here's a bit of real modern art for you. What do you make of it, sir?'

The mysterious circular apartment was exposed to their gaze, with its five open doors – the space within the fifth, last door still in wet paint and still uncompleted.

'It's some kind of allegory,' pronounced Cushman. 'The genre of the allegory has a perfectly respectable provenance in art history and is by no means confined only to the wilder shores of what you call modern art.' He pointed to the first door, the left-hand door. 'That could be a portrait of the dead husband. He's fair-haired like the child.'

'That's Giles, all right,' confirmed Orville, 'there's a picture of him on file. And that's Mrs Hawksmoor, I checked up on her in Press Clippings. She's reckoned to be one of the outstanding artists of her generation, did you know that, sir? You wouldn't say she's flattered herself in this picture, would you?'

Cushman was regarding Kate Hawksmoor's self-portrait in the second door, with head on one side, eyes narrowed. 'It certainly makes no concessions to prettifying,' he declared, 'but there's something there – something that shines through. I don't know what it is. Not yet.'

'Just like a picture-strip, isn't it?' said Orville, pointing. 'The next one up shows the kid as a new-born babe. And see, sir, there's Giles Hawksmoor again, looking back over his shoulder. Very rum.' His finger travelled to the right, and he gave a long, low whistle. 'Pheeew! Who's the bird in the nude with a baby – a boy baby, you're left in no doubt about *that*, are you?'

'The woman looks a bit of a fidget to me,' said Cushman. 'Built more for speed than for comfort.'

'I wonder who she is?' said Orville. 'Not someone that Mrs Hawksmoor likes very much, wouldn't you say, sir?'

'Very perceptive of you, Mark,' said his chief. 'Now that you mention it, this is not a flattering portrait, in spite of the fact that the artist hasn't pulled any punches with what might be described as the sitter's more obvious physical attractions. The inner bitch shines through. Yes, this lady – if she indeed exists – looks the sort who wouldn't hesitate to tell us a few revealing things about Mrs H. And what have we here . . . ?'

'A clifftop!' exclaimed Orville. '*The* clifftop!'

The last door was open wide. They were looking out on to a moonlit clifftop in teeming rain. The moonlight appeared to be an artistic device, merely, to illuminate the face of a woman who was shown in the act of pushing a bulky suitcase over the edge of the cliff. But the head was incomplete; no more than a flesh-coloured blob surrounded by a dark aureole of windswept hair.

'Is this going to be another self-portrait?' mused Cushman.

Their glances met.

By this time, the well-tried procedures of search and investigation were being carried out in Kate Hawksmoor's luxury studio flat. Every room had received a cursory going-over and was now being taken apart: floorboards were being raised and samples of dust removed for microscopic examination; waste-paper baskets emptied and their contents mulled over; sink traps, cisterns, the solid fuel cooking stove in the well-appointed kitchen, the very dustbin in the yard – all subjected to the closest attention. Within half an hour, the young pathologist in charge put his head through the door of the studio room.

'No signs,' he said.

'Blood?'

'Not a spot. This is only a preliminary, but, unless it was carried out with great expertise, there's been no dismemberment. I'll give you that in writing later this afternoon, when I've checked through the samples again in the lab.'

'Thanks, Doctor,' nodded Cushman.

Orville wrinkled his nose, for his superior's pipe smoke lay in still, plane clouds in the hot air. 'There didn't have to be dismemberment,' he said. 'A three-year-old's body could easily be crammed into a suit-case that size.' He pointed to the item in the painting. 'By the way, sir, the milkman says that Mrs Hawksmoor put out a note that he was only to leave one bottle a day in future.'

'Did she, now?' said Orville, puffing out a cloud. 'If a murderess, then a prudent and penny-watching murderess. Anything else turn up, Mark?'

Orville thumbed through a sheaf of reports that had just been sent in from the kitchen, where a communications room had been established. 'Something else from the informative milkman,' he said. 'It appears there was a daily woman here for a short while last year. Name of Holbein or Holdheim. She was a widow, and the milkman actually tried to date her. Then one day she wasn't here, and he never saw her again.'

'Have that woman found,' said Cushman. 'She'll be able to give us some background on the relationship between the mother and the child.' He walked over to the full-length portrait that stood against the wall. 'You know, the more I look at this kiddy's expression, the more I'm convinced that there's something wrong with her.'

Orville joined him by the picture; regarding it with head on one side. 'Wrong – in what sort of way, sir?' he asked. 'You mean not quite right in the head? Mentally handicapped?'

'I get the feeling that the artist is trying to say something of the kind,' declared Cushman. 'That's the remarkable thing about Mrs Hawksmoor's work: her curious ability to evoke images beyond outer appearances. Have we managed to get on to the family doctor yet?'

'They don't have a regular GP in London, sir. And

the little girl's birth was registered in Tunbridge
Wells, which is the nearest centre to Goudley.'

'Someone must have attended Mrs Hawksmoor when
she was carrying the child.'

'That's right, sir. Fellow named Dr Forbes-Bryce, of
Tunbridge Wells. Now deceased. He hadn't much of a
practice and it died with him.'

Cushman smote his brow. 'Someone must know if
the child was *compos mentis* or not,' he said. 'What about
the Brierleys? Did they imply anything of the sort when
they were questioned?'

'No, sir,' said Orville. 'Beyond some remark to the
effect that she took after her father. And they said it in
that sort of way – you know? They don't like Mrs
Hawksmoor.'

'Have them questioned again, Mark. Have it put to
them quite unequivocally, the real nitty-gritty: was the
child Priscilla mentally or physically handicapped in
such a way as to drive her mother to a mercy-killing?'

'Right away, sir,' said Orville.

'And Mark . . .'

'Sir?'

'Get on to Dr Manners. Throw the book at him. I
want a complete and verbatim report of the conversation between him and Mrs Hawksmoor on the occasion
of their last meeting. Hippocratic Oath or no Hippocratic Oath, I want to know what she said, apart from
accusing him of spying on her. And, since he is of the
opinion her problem is a psychological problem, ask
him if, in his opinion, she has the psychology of a
murderess.'

Orville left the study. His chief relit his pipe and sauntered towards the archway that led to the upper floor of the flat. He had been that way before; something other than purely professional interest drew him back there again. He entered Kate Hawksmoor's bedroom, crossed over to her dressing-table, where stood an exquisite Meissen figurine of a shepherdess: panniered skirts sprigged all over with tiny gold *fleurs de lys*; the lush of springtime on the perfectly modelled, upturned face.

'Perfection,' he said aloud. 'Of course, she can afford perfection. Apart from that, as an artist, she might reject any other. You never know. Would she destroy anything that was imperfect? I wouldn't – don't. But she – whether as artist or a woman with a psychological problem – I wonder . . .'

A carriage clock on the bedside table tinkled the hour of three. Cushman swore under his breath.

'Where *are* you, Mrs Hawksmoor?' he murmured.

The last of London's anonymous suburbs was behind her and she was journeying along the straight road that bisects the longest length of Epping Forest, where the trees on each side rise in green glory. A roe deer came out of the undergrowth, every sinew quivering for flight; turned and fled back into cover when it saw the red car coming up out of the heat haze.

Kate had opened all the windows and taken off the navy scarf, so that her hair streamed in unchecked abandonment. Behind the dark glasses, her eyes never strayed from a distant point in the road ahead. Behind her eyes, her mind roved freely over the events of the previous three years.

Pussy . . .

Strange, how the child had never responded to her in the way she had hoped. All that love gone to waste, all the bright dreams turned to water in her hands. Only once – on that idyllic day at the Zoo – had she come near to penetrating the child's carapace of reserve and suspicion . . .

'We'll go to Goudley, you'd like that, wouldn't you? We'll leave dusty old London and live in the country.'

'There's naminals in the country.'

'All sorts, darling. Cows and pigs, chickens and ducks. Ducks are such fun – so pompous, strutting like dowager duchesses at a Palace reception. And ponies. You could have a pony in Goudley. Learn to ride, for you're quite old enough to sit in a saddle and be taken out on a leading rein. Would you like that?'

'A white pony?'

'A white pony.'

The child had thrown her arms about her then; soft cheek against hers, warm body pressed close. Then, suddenly, she had stiffened, and the tiny limbs had threshed; small, bunched fists beating.

'Go away from me! I want my Daddy!'

'Darling . . .' (How to express it?) '. . . Daddy's gone to the angels. You never knew him.'

And then – clouding even that sweet, brief moment of rapport – the horror had begun all over again.

CHAPTER X

A YOUNG CONSTABLE had made himself at home in Kate
Hawksmoor's kitchen and had found the makings of a
pot of tea. He brought it into the studio room, set upon
a Georgian silver tray, with the single bottle of fresh
milk which had been delivered that morning perched
incongruously beside it.

'Nothing much to eat, sir,' he informed Cushman.
'Nothing but a few dry biscuits. Would you like to me
go out and get something? Anything you fancy?'

The phone rang by Cushman's elbow.

'Detective Chief Superintendent Cushman speaking.'

'There's a bakery on the King's Road,' said the
earnest young constable. 'They'll have sausage rolls
and . . .'

'Shut up!' snarled Cushman. 'No, not you, you fool!
What was that you said . . .?'

The young constable placed the tray close by his
master's hand, hovered reverently and indecisively for
a few moments – while the other listened at the receiver
with face growing perceptibly angrier by the instant –
and silently took his leave.

'Who is he – is he clean?' demanded Cushman of the
speaker at the other end. 'Is he, by God? Yes, let him
go by all means. What? Keep it there. No, better –
have it brought round here. Thanks.' He slammed
down the instrument, smote his brow with the palm of

his hand. 'Inspector Orville!' he bellowed.

Orville came running.

'Sir?'

'They've found the Rolls.'

'And Mrs Hawksmoor?'

'No Mrs Hawksmoor. The car was in the charge of a fellow named Carter, who claims to be in the process of purchasing the vehicle from her. Seems she gave him permission this morning to drive it around for as long as he chose.'

'It's a thin story, sir. How come it took us so long to find him if he was just driving it around?'

'After a short drive around,' said Cushman, 'he took it to see a coach body builder in Chelsea, about fixing the repair to the damage that Mrs Hawksmoor made to the front end. Our chaps picked him up a quarter of an hour ago as he drove out of a mews in the King's Road.'

'Or he's lying,' said Orville flatly.

'Maybe,' conceded his superior. 'But, since it appears that his father is a Privy Councillor and retired High Court Judge, I am willing – for the time being and in the interests of my pension – to give him the benefit of the doubt.'

'Did they get anything off him? – about Mrs Hawksmoor, I mean.'

'Nothing. He says he only met her the once. And again this morning when she chucked him the keys of the car out of the window,' replied Cushman. 'By the way, I told them to send the Rolls round here. I want that car gone over with a fine tooth-comb, particularly the boot. I want those pathologist boys to tell me everything she's carried in that boot in the last twelve months. What are you hopping from one foot to the other for, Mark? You look like a pregnant hen. What've you got to tell me?'

Orville grinned. 'I waved a thick stick at Dr Manners just now,' he said, 'and he's not the kind of feller who takes very kindly to the thick stick treatment. However, when I warned him that there was a chance of charges being proffered, he unbent a little.'

'Go on.'

'After Mrs Hawksmoor accused him of spying on her – that was when he enquired about the kid – she burst into tears and told him to leave her alone. And then she said – and I quote her, just as the doc gave it to me: "*I only did what had to be done, sooner or later!*" ' He gave the quotation a dramatic emphasis and awaited its effect upon his chief. Nor was he disappointed.

'And Manners has never seen Priscilla?'

'Never, sir.'

'So Mrs Hawksmoor's remark meant nothing particular to him. No indication of criminal behaviour, I mean. Like – she could have meant: "I had to send that bloody kid away to her auntie's because sooner or later she'll drive me out of my mind with her hollering" – something like that. Yes?'

Orville looked impressed. 'That's more or less exactly what he *did* think she meant,' he said. 'And that's why he didn't feel it incumbent upon him to tell me the first time. Because it related to Mrs Hawksmoor's psychological problems, her threatened nervous breakdown – as he thought.'

Cushman produced two photographs and laid them on the table.

'I found these in Mrs Hawksmoor's dressing-table drawer,' he said. 'They show her and the kid hand in hand. Not very good pictures. One of them was taken by a street tout outside the Zoo. Have them blown up and sent out to the Press. I want them on the front pages of tonight's editions.'

Orville gazed critically at the photos. 'They won't reproduce very well in newsprint,' he declared. 'Too grey. Why not use Mrs Hawksmoor's own representation of herself, sir? The face in the doorway. And why not use a head and shoulders of the kid from her mother's painting of her?'

'Good thinking, Mark,' said Cushman. 'Have our chaps photograph the paintings right away and get them off. Tell the editors that we're calling for their co-operation in this matter, and that the captions should read – ' He sketched a broad line in the air – ' "HAVE YOU SEEN THIS MOTHER AND CHILD?" '

Orville left the studio. Alone again, Cushman poured himself another cup of tea and carried it over to the portrait of the child Pussy, upon which he gazed ruminatively for some while, afterwards panning towards Kate Hawksmoor's representation of herself in the second doorway. Coloured for happiness, but with a cloud in the sky no bigger than a man's hand.

'Have I got it right, Mrs Hawksmoor?' he asked aloud. 'Is that the way it was? You put up with it for three years. Tragically widowed, then delivered of a

child who was maybe normal to the rest of the world –
to the Brierleys, maybe even the village doctor, who
saw her once in a while for measles and mumps. But
you, and perhaps only you, knew that she was fatally
flawed – flawed in the way you tried to express it in the
picture: a Meissen shepherdess with a broken-off head
that had been badly stuck back on again with glue –
like the one I've got back home in Bromley. I love that
bit of Meissen, Mrs Hawksmoor. But could you, with
your artist's instinct for perfection, with your psychological problems, love a little Meissen shepherdess with
a badly-stuck-back-on-again head enough to want to
keep her?'

A pause, and then a fresh thought obtruded: 'Or,
maybe, did you love her too much, so that you had to
destroy her for her own good?'

Another pause: 'And bury her at sea – symbolically
– in the place where the father met his end.'

And again: 'Where are you now, Mrs Hawksmoor?'

She had instinctively avoided the motorway, it being a
place of people and activity; the old main road,
reduced by Progress to its original role of country
highway, was more in accord with her mood and
feelings. Travelling at a steady forty miles an hour, she
made good headway along the winding, tree-shaded
ribbon of tarmac that led her north-eastwards to her
goal. Presently, when the motorway ran out and the
rest of the traffic was diverted back to the old main
road, she was dismayed to find herself stuck behind a
vast juggernaut that emitted clouds of diesel fumes

upon her and reduced her progress to a crawling pace on hills; nor was her ordeal made any easier by a similarly massive vehicle that closed in behind her and seemed intent upon forcing her under the giant wheels of the juggernaut in front.

Cast away from her private thoughts by the exigencies of maintaining the Mini on the road, Kate was bound to address herself to sundry practicalities: things like adjusting the rear-view mirror so that she could see how near the monster behind was to colliding with her; making sure that she had not omitted to cancel her flasher. In the course of doing all which, she saw to her alarm that the Mini was out of – or within a whisker of being out of – petrol. Almost immediately after she had registered this fact, a large service station complex loomed up on her nearside, dressed overall with flags of all nations and assorted bunting, with jumbo-sized posters announcing cut price offers and free gifts. She cut swiftly out of line and entered the complex – yet not swiftly enough to avoid a blast of horn from the following juggernaut for not signalling her intention.

Palms sweating, she awaited the arrival of the pump attendant: a pasty-faced youth with acne.

' 'Ow many?'

'Er – I'm sorry, but I don't know how many this car takes,' faltered Kate.

The youth rolled his eyes and muttered something that sounded like 'Women's Lib'. 'What's your petrol gauge say, missus?' he asked wearily.

'It's empty,' said Kate.

'Four gallons will do you,' said the youth, and proceeded to provide the petrol.

Kate cast a fearful glance about her. She had not bargained for stopping on her north-eastward odyssey, nor to put to hazard her resolve by delay or contact with others. The bodkin in her handbag suddenly seemed like a bad joke. In a bustling service station, surrounded by flags of all nations and family motorcars, caravans stuck all over with badges betokening that the happy owners have visited Benidorm, Longleat Lion Park, Pamplona, Blackpool Illuminations, does one live comfortably with the notion that one is travelling to murder one's husband's former lover, on the assumption – God, how loosely assembled the notion in retrospect! – that the said lover had herself murdered one's husband?

It was then she saw the police. They were in a white Range-Rover whose sleek sides were banded with lurid red stripes outlined in blue. Two men in the front seats. One of them sitting with his peaked cap tipped forward on his nose, his head resting back against the high support; he could have been asleep. His companion – the driver – was examining his teeth in the rear-view mirror. Kate relaxed. Surely no danger there.

'Okay, missus, that'll be – er – three pounds twelve to you – but I'd charge double to anyone else.' He leered, showing broken and discoloured teeth. Clearly, he had reconsidered Kate, and cast aside the Women's Lib aspect.

She drew breath sharply, while delving into her handbag.

'I haven't got any money! Do you take credit cards?'

'Of course, missus,' said the youth, peering over the door sill and probing with lugubrious sheep's eyes into the contents of her crocodile skin handbag.

She proffered a card.

'You take it to the office, missus,' he said, pointing.

'Oh no!'

The way to the glass-screened cash desk lay past the front of the parked police car!

The youth opened the door for her.

'Please,' she said. 'Will you deal with this for me? Take the card and fix everything, I mean.'

He spread his long white hands. 'I got me work to do, missus,' he said. 'I work the pumps, her in the office handles the change and fixes the cards.' He turned and shouted: 'Four gallons of three star here, Nellie. Three pounds twelve. Okay?'

Kate snatched up the navy scarf and hastily knotted it under her chin. A glance at herself in the mirror – white-faced in dark glasses and wimple – and she stepped out of the car. The way to the beckoning cash desk was like a walk to the scaffold, with surely a hundred pairs of eyes upon her: a woman on her way to murder. And in a stolen car at that. God, why had she been such an impulsive fool as to take the Mini?

The two policemen in the Range-Rover never so much as glanced at the woman in the dark glasses and headscarf throughout her transaction at the cash window. The driver continued to attend to his teeth, picking away at the incisors with the end of a matchstick. His companion remained with his head back, cap tipped low over his nose.

On their return from Goudley, and the subsequent questioning by the police, Cynthia Brierley had, as she put it, 'steadied her nerves with a couple of snifters' and then spent the greater part of the afternoon sunning herself in the patio of her Spanish-style bungalow in Mill Hill. Her figure – svelte still, despite a tendency to a thickness of the upper arms – showed to advantage in a bikini, and gleamed with oil. She lay in a chaise-longue, close by the kidney-shaped pool, in whose brilliant blue depths a mechanical contrivance of disturbingly anthropoid appearance was slowly creeping around the bottom, sucking up unconsidered fragments and wiping the corners out with its long, sweeping tail. By Cynthia's side, a cassette-player had just run out of a selection from Vivaldi ('Gems from Vivaldi'), whom the Brierleys knew to be a very in-type composer.

Colin Brierley registered the fact of his wife's sleeping state from the window of his 'snug' that overlooked the patio; which done, he tiptoed over to the telephone and slowly dialled a South London number. A woman's voice answered it.

'It's Colin,' he whispered.

'Darling – I can hardly hear you.'

'I've got to speak quietly, I'm ringing from home. Listen, darling, and listen carefully. The balloon's about to go up.'

'Oh no!'

'Yes. My last hope has just flown out of the window. As soon as the banks open their doors on Monday morning, I'm done for. So I'm pulling out while the going's good.'

'You're taking me with you! You're not leaving me behind to face the music!'

'Now, would I do that to my darling girl? Listen – meet me at the Air France counter at Heathrow at six. At six, got it? And bring all my things – the clothes and things at your place. That means I can leave here empty-handed and not cause any comment.'

'Oh, darling! I can't believe it's happening. That we're going away together at last.'

'Sure, sure. It's really great. Don't forget my things. And don't forget to bring all the money you can lay hands on. See you at six.'

'I'll be there, my darling.'

' 'Bye, then.'

'*Dah*-ling . . .'

'Mmmm? Yes?'

'Haven't we sort of forgotten something?'

'Ah, yes. Who's Colly's baby dolly then?'

'I Colly's baby dolly, and I want cuddles.'

'That's great. Great. See you at six.' Brierley replaced the telephone – gently, so as to reduce to the minimum the faint tinkle of the bell when the cradle was depressed – and tiptoed out of his 'snug', closing the door behind him.

Outside on the patio, Cynthia Brierley, who had had her ear pressed close by the Spanish-style window during the greater part of her husband's whispered delivery, raised her head and stared into the middle distance with an expression of feline malevolence.

'You bastard!' she hissed. 'You dirty, double-dealing bastard! I'll fix your little game, see if I don't!'

The incident of the service station had greatly un-nerved Kate; it had served as an intrusion upon the tight carapace of privacy that she had woven about her sensibilities. Upon making the resolve to kill Zoë Chalmers, she had become her own woman, a creature apart, a mind pledged to a course of action. Now she discovered herself to be a frightened, muddle-headed, hysterical thing who had not even had the sense to hire a motor-car to journey to East Anglia, but had prob-ably brought down upon herself the attention of the entire constabulary of southern England. It followed, then, that she must take steps to minimize the mess she had made for herself by reducing the chances of meet-ing up with the police again. The officers in the Range-Rover, she was sure, had not paid the slightest attention to either the car or to herself. She could not rely upon her good luck to continue. Accordingly, she pulled in at the next lay-by and consulted the pocket map she had brought with her.

Tracing the road to the village of Wingham (shall I find you arranging the flowers and polishing the altar brasses, Zoë?) Kate discovered that, by taking a right hand turn a mile or so ahead from where she was parked, she could, by following a tortuous course from village to village, entirely avoid the market towns of Saffron Walden, Newmarket and Bury St Edmunds,

which, on a Saturday afternoon in high summer, must
surely be packed with traffic, shoppers, tourists – and
police. It was simply a matter, she told herself, of
tackling the problem in the sort of way that a cater-
pillar eats a leaf: begin by nibbling away at one corner,
progressing, bit by bit, till one has reached the other
side; or, in other words, to navigate cross-country the
way in which the rough-riding steeplechasers of the
eighteenth century had used to do: by fixing one's
gaze upon the next church steeple. One problem at a
time. Patience wins out.

Tossing the map on to the seat beside her, Kate
switched on the engine and set off on her steeplechase;
turned right at the next intersection, following the signpost to her first village, which rejoiced in the charming
name of Toppers Hall Green.

She never positively located Toppers Hall Green. A
stark clump of thatched barns, a dusty duckpond, three
staring children, a derelict tractor, a copse of high
beech trees resounding with the hooting cries of
hidden pigeons – that may have been Toppers Hall
Green. Two miles further on, Kate was confronted by
a fingerpost pointing down a narrow lane to a place
called East Ratting. Despairingly, she spun the wheel
and followed the way it pointed. A mile on, the narrow
lane became a single track that was presently overhung
with the snakey fingers of pollarded willows which
interlaced above and formed a tunnel of green gloom.
Near to panic, sobbing with despair and fright com-
bined, she carried on because there was no hope, no
real profit, in going back.

The nightmare ended with the brusque elegance of a well-told joke. The little red Mini debouched into a T-junction, and Kate stalled the engine while braking to avoid a procession of grave-faced school-children who were being shepherded along a dusty lane by a woman in a floral hat, who nodded affably at her and twinkled through rimless pebbled glasses.

There was a village – more like a hamlet – beyond the hedgerows. A fingerpost announced it to be: *Zule – 1 mile.*

Zule was not even on her map. Kate gave a sob of despair.

She was lost. Utterly and irretrievably lost in a green labyrinth of rural East Anglia.

CHAPTER XI

Two HOURS in Kate Hawksmoor's luxury studio flat, and Cushman unquestionably knew her better. Padding to and fro in his shirtsleeves, collar unbuttoned, a cup of tea in his hand, the detective became privy to the minutiæ of the absent owner's life in many unconsidered respects. He discovered, for instance, that, though she was obviously a cat lover (a collection of Louis Wain drawings in the hallway, a row of books devoted to matters feline), there was no sign of her possessing one as a pet. (Hay fever, or an allergy to cat fur?) He learned much about her eating habits (practically a vegetarian, and nothing out of tins), her wardrobe (mostly pretty, casual clothing), and the fact that she slept nude. But always he returned to the painting of the oval room as his centre of gravity in the summation of the enigma who was Kate Hawksmoor. That – and the perfect Meissen shepherdess.

Orville it was who brought him news that the run-away had been sighted. Orville was not bearing up well under the heat of the afternoon; Cushman noted with a touch of amused malice that the tall athlete was sweating badly.

'They found her! She was driving a stolen car! But they lost her!'

Cushman smote his brow. 'How in the hell could anyone . . .?'

'It was a patrol car of the Essex police on the A11,' said Orville. 'They were specifically looking for stolen cars, to get a line on a North London gang that has been shipping the merchandise across to Holland via the East Coast ports. Only minutes before our Mrs Hawksmoor pulled into a garage for a fill-up, they got the report on the number and description of the Mini she was driving. It had been knocked off from a mews just round the corner from here.'

'And yet they didn't pick up the stolen Mini?'

'Their orders were to observe and report,' said Orville. 'They passed the information on to the chain of patrol cars strung out along the routes to the coast. As soon as Mrs Hawksmoor had driven out of the filling station, they checked with the cashier about the credit card with which she'd paid for the petrol. Then they knew she was the woman we're all looking for. But by that time it was too late.'

'She'd gone to ground?'

'Certainly left the main road, sir,' said Orville. 'And you know what darkest Essex is like.'

'Damn!' growled his superior, groping for his pipe. And again: 'Damn. That woman seems to have a charmed life as far as we're concerned, Mark. First we go chasing that confounded Rolls all over London, then we let her pinch a car right under our noses and sneak off to Essex. And now – this!'

'Wonder why Essex?' mused Orville.

Cushman pointed his pipe at his subordinate. 'We'll find out,' he said. 'Get on to it. Has she any relations in East Anglia whom she might reasonably

expect to hide her? Check back on the dead husband.
Round up the fellows who were his business associates.
Put someone on to the insurance company who paid out
on that quarter of a million claim. A quarter of a
million pay-out hurts, and they won't have parted
company with it without a lot of snooping around.
Maybe they found something that smelt – but not
enough to give them grounds to contest the claim.
Most of all, find out if either Mrs Hawksmoor or her
dead husband have or had any connections in East
Anglia. And what news from the Brierleys? Did they
give you anything new on the child's state of health?'

Orville brightened. 'I was coming to that, sir,' he
said. 'Before we had time to ring them, Mrs Brierley
rang us. In a state of hysteria. Brierley's left home.'

'Has he, now? Is that of any interest to us?'

'It might be, sir. In view of the impending enquiries into his business carryings-on, if for nothing
else. Particularly since he's aiming to skip the country.'

Cushman raised an eyebrow. 'You had that from the
wife? She's very co-operative, I must say. There has to
be another woman in the case.'

Orville nodded. 'There is, sir. Brierley's meeting the
other woman at Heathrow at six. His wife overheard
him making the assignation over the phone.'

'See that we have a reception committee there to
greet him at six. And did you get anything out of Mrs
Brierley about the child?'

'By the time she'd finished putting the boot into her
husband, she was raving,' said Orville. 'Sounded as if

she'd fortified herself at the gin bottle before she rang in. I could get no sense out of her.'

'Tell the reception committee,' said Cushman. 'Have them put the question to Brierley at the airport, first off. Was there anything odd about Pussy?'

It was the first time either of the detectives had used little Priscilla Hawksmoor's pet name.

The village of Zule beckoned, for the afternoon sun cast long, eastward-pointing shadows towards it. The procession of children and their floral-hatted shepherdess fairly filled the lane in front of the Mini and showed no inclination to move aside and let it pass. A little further on, passing a high-hedged cottage garden, three more children ran out to join the procession. Like the rest, they were dressed in their best: all neatly-pressed, with shining boots and polished hair, clean faces and bright eyes. Kate dropped into bottom gear and resigned herself to bringing up the tail end.

Zule was no more than a steepled church, one rutted village street, weatherboarded cottages, an open green space with a duckpond, a public house called the Essex Arms. And it was seething with people. They stood against the walls of the surrounding cottages and were packed forward to the edge of the green. They hung like grapes from the branches of the willows that part overhung the duckpond. They filled the narrow windows right up to the dormers in the roofs. A thousand regarding, bucolic faces marked the arrival of Kate Hawksmoor to their midst; while she, appalled to find her way suddenly blocked behind and before, stalled her engine and huddled herself in the seat, wide-eyed and breathless with apprehension.

The most alarming aspect was the total silence. Not even the children with whom Kate had processed added their jot of chatter as, reaching their goal, they broke their files and melted into the crowd. A thousand patient, still folk, country people all, in their Sunday best. Standing. Waiting.

Presently, the crowd stirred. A hum of excitement spread through the open space surrounding the green. Kate Hawksmoor's unease increased. She had the notion to leap out of the car and abandon it to the people of Zule; to run away into the silent, concealing lanes – anywhere, to distance herself from whatever it was that the people waited and watched for.

They came . . .

First, the tap-tap of a drum or tambour. Then, the thin jingle of small, massed bells sounding in counter-point. Next, a sketchy tune played upon a sort of penny whistle. This was taken up and augmented by a concertina. The crowd sighed. Parted.

They came from the lane behind the church, towards the green. Dancing, swaying, advancing two steps and retiring one step; moving with a deliberate and patterned slowness, to the tune and beat of tambour, whistle and concertina. Six men in white flannel, straw hatted and garlanded with summer flowers in red, white and blue, hung about with ribbon tails and bearing hawthorn sticks. And with every dancing step they stamped out the rhythm with the massed silver bells tied below their knees. Morris Men of rural England.

Kate relaxed in her seat and wiped her damp palms. Morris dancing she regarded as a pleasant anachronism of the kind that only the English could have devised. The costume of dubious provenance: tarted-up cricket gear. And, surely, if the complicated figure that was being performed by the six nameless men derived from pre-history, an obscure atavistic folk memory, why in Victorian boaters? She resigned herself to a – hopefully – short delay in her eastward odyssey of vengeance (Await me, Zoë, in Church Gate Cottage, all in serene ignorance of my coming. For coming I am!).

The dancers reached the green. The tune changed, became less catchy and attractive; took on a more primitive, abandoned rhythm. The Morris Men's heads swung low on their turns. Their waving arms flapped lifelessly, like the arms of animated scarecrows. Adding to their abandonment, a creature in a mockery of female attire – his bearded face enveloped in a poke bonnet, his hairy legs emerging from the hem of a flowered skirt – proceeded to belabour the dancers about their heads with an inflated bladder on a stick and string, urging them on to attend to the niceties of their steps. Kate experienced a return of her unease, recalling that, beyond her slightly patronizing acceptance of Morris dancing as a picturesque fragment of the rural scene, there had always been, in her mind, something indefinably *sinister* about the whole thing, something that even the seedy cricketing gear and the absurd hats could not quite dispel, some true vein of

displayed atavism that was as real and raw as the
stench of the big cat house at the Zoo.

Nor was the rawness but half begun. The dancers,
simulating – or genuinely experiencing? – a sudden
lassitude, sank to the grass and lay there like dead men,
while the fool with the stick and bladder ambled away,
cackling with eldritch laughter.

Impulsively, Kate clutched at the wheel of the Mini.
The people's faces – they were pressing close about the
little car, and they were displayed all round her, save
ahead, where the green lay – had taken on a new
expectancy. Glazed eyes stared, slack-lipped mouths
hung open. A woman seized at a small child and drew
it close to her side. A man with the high-cheek-
boned look of a Viking swallowed hard so that his
Adam's apple rose and fell like a ballcock. And the
tambour took up a slow beat, the other instruments
falling silent.

Through the open window, Kate heard the people
whisper, one to the other.

'He's comin'.'

'Watch out for the hobby-horse!'

'The hobby-horse!'

It came with the tambour man leading: a grotesque
and unseemly shape that in no way suggested horse;
but was more like some monstrous beetle, or wood-
louse, with a rudimentary head set at one end.
Fashioned of ancient, cracked leather attached to a
supporting frame, with a leather skirt around its lower
edge, the thing was carried by a man concealed beneath
it; all that could be seen of him was his bare feet and

the lower ends of a pair of remarkably well-muscled legs. In time to the tambour, this thing, the hobby-horse, advanced in whirling, darting motion along the edge of the crowd, which fell back at its approach, as one will avoid any noxious creature. Yet there was also, among some of the people – among the women, and more particularly among the young girls – a half-hesitant yielding to the temptation of retreat; almost as if they welcomed the advances of the strange apparition, but were constrained from accepting them through the fear of being thought too forward.

Huddled in her seat, hemmed in by the crowds on each side and behind, Kate watched the advance of the gyrating thing; saw it pause, turn, seem to look around, and light upon a young girl – a pretty creature in a white dress, with flowers in her corn-coloured hair – who was standing in the front row of the crowd, gazing upon the hobby-horse with eyes half-frightened, half-wanton. The thing took a step nearer, and it seemed that the girl must back away and hide herself among the people; instead, she stood her ground, which won her the admiration of the crowd, who cheered her, clapped hands, waved handkerchiefs. She stood her ground, still, when the thing of wood and leather with the man beneath reared up before her. A bare hand and arm reached out from the shadowed interior, took hold of the girl's wrist and dragged her, not entirely unresisting, inside the body of the hobby-horse. The crowd roared its delight; only the girl's companion – he looked to be her brother or her sweet-heart – seemed not to approve; he watched the hobby-horse, which was now standing still, with surly eyes and pouting lip. A full minute passed before the victim was released from under the hobby-horse, which immediately bounded away in a very sprightly manner leaving the girl with the corn-coloured hair facing the laughter of the crowd and the anxious looks of her companion. She was pink-cheeked, breathless, dishevelled.

Two more females were chosen by the hobby-horse for its attentions: one a mere girl like the first, the other a mature woman of handsome face and figure. Both emerged from their ordeal in some confusion of looks, both won high approval from the crowd. The thing continued on its way, the tambour man following.

Kate's fingers tightened on the steering-wheel. She had the wild idea to start the engine and drive off across the green, risking the disaster of crashing through the press of people at the far side, or of ending up in the duckpond. She even reached blindly for the ignition, fumbled the key and dropped it. In the act of reaching down to pick it up, she saw to her horror that the hobby-horse was closing down upon her.

'Hob! Hob! Come on, Hob!' The people were shouting all round her.

'Come on, hoss!'

'Here's a fine young maid!'

Someone opened the car door. The crowd fell back and left a space all round. The prancing thing of wood and leather made a complete circle of the red Mini, in which cowered its intended victim.

'Go it, Hob! Take her, lad!'

Kate fought to close the car door, but laughing

youths dragged it open again. One of them reached inside to pull her out into the waiting arms of the bare-legged creature under the monstrosity of wood and leather. She – who had a morbid terror both of en-closed spaces and of being manhandled – fought back like a tigress, raking the clutching hands with her fingernails. It was then she remembered that she was armed, and groped for her handbag, fumbled inside it for the needle-pointed bodkin, found it and took it out. Bag in one hand, bodkin in the other, she clambered out of the car and faced her tormentors, who fell back in alarm, to see the glittering point jutting from her small fist, and read the wild determination in the eyes of the terrified woman.

No one – not even the man under the hobby-horse – raised a finger to stop her as she stumbled away across the green, walking backwards, the bodkin out-thrust in protection. No one uttered a sound. And when she reached the far side of the open space, the crowd parted to let her through. Clear of the people, Kate then turned and ran – up the rutted village street, past the church and on; till, presently, the place called Zule was be-hind her, no more than a steeple raised above the trees. That and a nightmare memory.

And the high-hedged lanes of the rural labyrinth stretched on before her into an infinity of mysteries.

Three more police vehicles – among them a fully-equipped radio van – were by now parked in the se-cluded drive of Kate Hawksmoor's luxury studio flat, a circumstance which excited attention even in that highly conservative residential area. A small crowd had formed near the gate: two uniformed nannies with prams, a dark-skinned man in a tarboosh, an elderly lady with a Pomeranian on a leash, two awed school-girls, and a man in tweeds and a cheese-cutter cap. Nor were they to be shifted, despite the repeated demands from the uniformed constable guarding the entrance; but craned their necks to peer into every vehicle that arrived, speculating among themselves who and what they might contain. The rumour started, and was speedily established throughout the neighbourhood, that a terrorist – or terrorists – was barricaded up in the attic floor of the building and was holding a child as hostage. Why else all the frantic comings and goings of the police?

Alex Cushman saw the small crowd of onlookers from the studio window. He lowered the curtain and grunted.

'What time will the evening papers with our pictures be on the street?' he demanded.

'Some time between six and seven, sir,' replied Orville.

'Not that they're going to be of any immediate use,' said Cushman. 'Not now. No one in darkest East Anglia sees the London evening papers. Best get the pictures shown on TV. See to it right away, will you, Mark? Ask for a flash on all the news channels starting from now.'

'Right away,' said Orville.

The phone rang. It was Cushman's wife, calling for the second time, to check if he would be coming to their daughter's birthday treat, a visit to the theatre, after all. He told her no. Immediately following that, a runner from the radio van outside came in with a report that the stolen red Mini had been found abandoned in a remote Essex village called Zule; not by the village policeman, for they were a thing of the past, but by an officer in a patrolling Panda car, who had been making a routine check on certain heathenish carryings-on that had taken place in the said village on the third Saturday in August since time immemorial.

Cushman drove his fist into the palm of his other hand and swore.

'She's done it again! She's given us the slip. While ever she hung on to that Mini, we were bound to find her sooner or later. Now where do we start to look?'

At about this same time, a plainclothes officer noted for his tact and persuasion (qualities that, as many villains had learned too late and to their cost, served only to mask a ruthlessness in the pursuit of truth) had run to earth the senior partner of the late Giles Hawksmoor's firm of Lloyds brokers at the seventh tee of his expensive golf-course in North London, and had so impressed that prudent and cautious gentleman by his extensive knowledge of the more esoteric aspects of the noble and ancient game that the former was half inclined to speak freely about certain indiscretions committed by his late colleague.

Around about this time, also, another detective had located, aboard a 30-foot yawl moored at Burnham-on-Crouch, the boss of the top-flight private enquiry agency who had handled – and with exemplary discretion – the probe into the whys and wherefores of Giles Hawksmoor's end, for the insurance company who had paid out the claim. The owner of the yawl, fresh in from winning a deep water race that afternoon, was perfectly willing to co-operate. After calling upon the assistance of his visitor in the taking down of the sails and the squaring-off of the upper deck, he and his wife entertained the detective with pink gins in the narrow cabin below; where he gave his summation of the Giles Hawksmoor case, which was this: Hawksmoor's death was one of those once-in-a-million fatalities that defy chance and likelihood. He, personally, had thoroughly investigated the case, as a result of which enquiries he had reported that Giles Hawksmoor died as the result of a freak accident.

'Nothing fishy about it at all, old boy,' he concluded. 'Sheer rotten luck, that's all. Put it this way: if you were staging your own suicide to make it look like an accident so your missus could pick up the insurance, would you go to such unlikely lengths? Wouldn't you just drive hell-for-leather round some corner and into a convenient tree? Another gin, love? How about you, old boy?'

Dusty, footsore, confused, frightened, Kate rounded a bend in an interminable lane and saw a metalled road, with traffic flashing by, and a signpost indicating that Bishop's Stortford was a mere half-mile distant. She trudged the half-mile, trailing her handbag with its murder weapon, and had the prudence to stop and comb out the rats' tails of her hair and put on some lipstick before she entered the first garage that came up and enquired about a taxi. Yes, they could take her anywhere she wanted to go. Norfolk? Nothing easier. A cultured accent and a crocodile handbag inspire total confidence, particularly when allied to a lovely face and figure.

The car they provided was a Ford of dubious vintage, and its driver was of a similar mould: a large and collapsed party with egg stains on his hand-knitted pullover, a peaked cap, and a trail of nicotine reaching up from the corner of his mouth to his cheekbone. He introduced himself as Gerald and invited her to sit beside him in the front.

'Wingham, isn't it?' said Gerald. 'T'other side of Wymondham.'

'Yes,' she replied.

'Anywhere in particular in Wingham?'

'Just on the outskirts.' She had thought this through. 'Just outside the village. I – I always like to walk the last few yards. It's so – pretty.' She had never been to the place in her life.

They set off through the summer's afternoon, with the windows open, while Gerald chain-smoked and carried on a monologue about his life and times as a taxi-driver in the eastern counties, and about some of the diverse characters whom he had transported. Kate slipped easily into the private world inside her head.

It seemed important to concentrate upon the purpose of her journey. So much had happened since she had left London to obscure her resolve. Barring accidents, the road ahead would presently bring her to

Zoë Chalmers's door. There was almost no turning back. Was she still of a mood to carry out her intent? Later, when the time came, would she be able to go through with it? She would never know till the time came . . .

Something that Gerald said broke in on her thoughts. She glanced at him sharply.

'I expect you agree,' he said.

'I – I'm afraid I was wool-gathering,' she said.

'I was saying about kiddies. Like this one I have to take for treatment Thursdays. No more than a vegetable really. No sense in it if you ask me. I mean, the kiddie's a misery to herself and everybody round her. That poor woman, her mother, she's never known a day's peace since the creature was born, surely. Best if that sort was quietly put down I always say. Don't you think so?'

'NO!'

She almost screamed the denial. The driver bucked in his seat. The car swerved wildly into the middle of the road. Kate clenched her fists, driving the fingernails hard against her palms. She caught a glimpse of her reflection in the rear-view mirror: her face was white, the eyes staring, brimming with tears.

'I – I'm sorry, missus . . .' Gerald began.

'It's all right,' she whispered.

'Not very tactful of me, like. I spec' you've had some experience of the sort.'

'Yes,' she whispered. 'Yes, I have.'

'Kiddie of your own?'

She nodded.

'It's very hard,' said Gerald. 'Only child?'

'Can we please talk about something else?' she begged.

'Sure.'

He did not speak for a long while. By the time he had sufficiently recovered his composure, Kate was firmly inside her head, and with no thought of where she was and why she was. Only an aching emptiness.

CHAPTER XII

CUSHMAN TOOK OUT the pocket watch that had been presented to his father after twenty-five years' service on the railway. Six-fifteen.

'Brierley must have walked into the reception committee at Heathrow by now,' he said. 'Any other reports in, Mark?'

'Charles drew a blank in Burnham-on-Crouch,' said Orville. 'That was to be expected. The enquiry agents went through Giles Hawksmoor's comings and goings during his last days very thoroughly; where he stayed and so forth. All the factual stuff was very systematically gone into. How he died was pure speculation, and they plumped for the most likely option. Nothing there for us. No help at all.'

'No East Anglia connection?'

'Not a smell.'

'Pity,' said Cushman. 'Where, oh, where are you, Mrs Hawksmoor? And for why?'

The telephone rang.

'This could be the reception committee from Heathrow,' said Orville, picking up the receiver.

It was not; it was the tactful and persuasive officer who had spent the greater part of the afternoon with the senior partner of the late Giles Hawksmoor's firm. What he had to tell Orville sent the latter's ballpoint racing across the pages of his notebook, and caused

Cushman much frustration as he tried to piece together their conversation with the help of his subordinate's crabbed scribble, peering over the other's
shoulder and fidgeting from one foot to the other.

'What was that all about?' he demanded, when Orville put down the receiver. 'Joe is on to something
big – yes?'

'It might be the breakthrough,' said the other.

'Give it to me.'

'Giles Hawksmoor was running a bird. He had a
mistress at the time of his death.'

'That much I did gather,' said Cushman. 'I don't
have cloth ears. Does she have a name?'

'Zoë Chalmers,' said Orville, consulting his notebook. 'The senior partner, Eveleigh by name, helped
Hawksmoor to execute a settlement of ten thousand
a year on this woman.'

'Did he, by God?' said Cushman. And he whistled.
'Pheew. That's not a bad bundle of boodle. What else?'

'Eveleigh can't lead us to the Chalmers woman. The
name is all he has.'

'Lying?'

'Perhaps not, sir. Leastways, he put Joe on to another
partner in the firm who used to socialize with the
Hawksmoors, which he, Eveleigh, didn't. He in his
turn remembers a guy who used to go around with the
Chalmers woman. Fellow name of – let's see – Walker,
Peter J. Walker. Joe phoned him just now.'

'And?'

'Walker wasn't having any. Said he'd lost contact
with Zoë Chalmers after Hawksmoor's death, didn't

have her present address. Joe's of the opinion that he's lying. And he's going round to beard him in his den right away.'

'Joe will get the answer,' opined Cushman. 'Half an hour of our Joe and Walker will be pulling all his family skeletons out of the closet on display. Trouble is we need quick answers.' He tapped his pipe on his lower dentures, a habit that Orville found particularly irritating.

'We could . . .' began Orville.

'Back to Cornwall!' cried Cushman. 'Hawksmoor's comings and goings during his last days!'

'Which the enquiry agents – and our own people – investigated so thoroughly!'

'Only – they didn't know about the Chalmers woman.'

'Hotel registers! They could have been very discreet, sir. Not speaking to each other in public. Just two names in hotel registers.'

'Two names – *with addresses*!'

'If she *was* with him, sir . . .'

'If she *was* with him,' said Cushman, reflectively stroking his cheek with the smooth bowl of his pipe. 'And remember, Mark, that she didn't come forward at his death, or at the inquest . . .'

They outstared each other for a full half-minute.

'I'll get things moving right away, sir,' said Orville. 'We'll have the answer long before Joe gets Walker to unburden.'

He left. He had scarcely gone, Cushman had scarcely had time to get his pipe going nicely, when the phone rang again. This time it was indeed the officer in charge of the 'Reception Committee' who had been attending Colin Brierley's assignation with his lady friend at the Air France counter at Heathrow.

'What?' demanded Cushman. And then: 'I don't give a damn if he's swindled all the widows and orphans in Britain. Give that to the Fraud Squad. So he's singing like a canary. What did he have to say about the child? What about Pussy?'

A pause. Very deliberately and carefully, Cushman laid his pipe down upon the inlaid table top.

'Go on – yes?'

And then: 'Are you *sure* about that? Is that what he said?'

The question bringing an affirmative, Alex Cushman put down the receiver and met his own astonished reflection in Kate Hawksmoor's handsome Regency mirror.

Men were haymaking in the wide, flat meadows of Norfolk, under a Constable sky. Kate, who was inclined to hay fever, was obliged to shut the window on her side. They came at last to a level-crossing, where a straggling line of cars awaited the passing of an interminable string of coal wagons. Gerald switched off the engine and lit another cigarette from the butt of his last. A heavy silence hung between them.

She compressed her thoughts to the task ahead of her, and marvelled to find that she was so calm. Even the slender skewer of steel that lay in the bottom of her handbag did not have the power to evoke deep emotion.

She felt empty of feeling – as when all tears have been shed, all repining done. The dispassionate killer.

'Here we go,' said Gerald, restarting the engine. 'Wingham's just round the next bend, ain't it? You can see the church spire. Let me know when you want to be dropped off.'

The strange village announced itself by a roadside garage and a row of mean cottages. The church stood beyond a clump of sentinel cypresses.

'Please stop here,' said Kate, in a voice that did not sound like her own.

Gerald obeyed; got out and opened the door for her. She had paid the garage in advance with her credit card, and did not have even a few pence to offer him as a tip, which seemed churlish.

'You'll not be wanting me to wait?' he asked. 'Seeing as how you haven't got any luggage, I wondered, like.'

'Thanks, but I won't be needing you again,' said Kate. 'My – plans are rather vague,' she added lamely.

He nodded. Turned to get back into the car. Paused, and said: 'What we was talking about just now. About handicapped kiddies, I mean. They can do such clever things nowadays, the doctors can. Where there's life, there's hope. That kiddie of yours . . .'

'There's nothing can be done for her,' said Kate evenly. 'My daughter is dead. Killed.' Without another word, she turned and walked away down the village street, towards the spire that rose above the cypresses, where Church Gate Cottage must lie. And in her mind

rose the astonishing thought that it was to an almost
complete stranger – a commonplace, chain-smoking
taxi-driver with leanings towards compulsory eutha-
nasia for the deprived – that she had made her first
confession about Pussy.

Church Gate Cottage, as its name implied, was indeed
almost within the shadow of Wingham church spire.
It was set sideways-on to the road, with a high,
private hedge and two tall chimneys. Flint-faced in the
East Anglian style, its uncompromising greyness was
countered by a riot of colour from a herbaceous border
enclosing a small lawn. There was no sound but the
humming of bees.

Kate directed her hand to the gate. Saw it open to
her touch. Walked, as if in a dream, down a crooked,
crazy-paved path that led to an enclosed porch, where
a white-painted door stood ajar. Inside, she could see
the edge of a carpet, a well-waxed floor, a hint of
polished brassware. Something moved in there.

'Is that you, Stan?'

A click-click of wooden-soled shoes on parquet. A
tall figure, suavely rounded. Hair tied up in a Hermès
scarf. Eyes whose mild surprise was hidden behind
round, dark glasses.

'Oh, hello. I thought it was the fish man. He sometimes comes on . . .'

A slim, sun-tanned hand reached up and removed
the glasses. Kate looked into the eyes of her dead
husband's mistress, saw astonished recognition.

'Good God, it's you!' A pause, then: 'Well, come on in and have a drink while you're here.'

The room smelt of beeswax and potpourri. To her surprise, Kate found herself meekly taking a seat in a well-stuffed armchair covered in a Jacobean-patterned linen.

'Well, what brings you to this part of the world, Kate?'

Zoë's back was towards her. She was pouring drinks into long glasses and tumbling ice cubes from a pair of tongs. Very brisk, very assured and capable. The first shock of surprise had given way to – what? Amusement? Receiving no reply to her question, she did not repeat it, but uncapped a bottle of tonic water, filled up both glasses, tossed the discarded cap right across the room, to land exactly in the middle of the open fireplace in a bed of dead ash. The action seemed to please her. She smiled brightly at Kate as she came over with the glasses.

'Drinkies.'

'I don't want a drink,' whispered Kate hoarsely.

'Oh.' Zoë looked disconcerted for a moment. 'Well, I certainly do. Cheers.' The hand that lifted the long glass to her faultlessly painted lips surely gave a tremor.

'I know about – you and Giles,' said Kate.

Beautifully-shaped eyebrows rose in another display of mild surprise. 'Do you now? And who told you, pray?'

'I overheard.'

'One shouldn't eavesdrop,' declared Zoë. 'One does it to hear good things about oneself, of course. Generous and lovely things that other folk think about one. Such a pity that one only eavesdrops on to all the dirt. When did you hear?'

'Only the other day. Tuesday, I think it was.' Kate passed her hand across her brow. 'It seems – a long time ago now.'

'How did you find me?' asked Zoë. 'I've been out of circulation for quite a while now.'

'Peter Walker told me your address.'

'Did he now?' Two small, vertical lines suddenly appeared – revealing as the first white-capped wavelet on a calm ocean – in the centre of Zoë's perfect brow. 'Did he now? Very – *informative* – of him! And so, you've come to confront the Scarlet Woman, is that it?'

Kate said: 'I think I've come to kill you.'

The smile on the painted lips wavered – but only for an instant. 'My dear! Such dramatics. You know, I really think you do need this drink after all. No? Well, it won't be wasted.' She tipped the contents of the second glass into her own.

'One thing I must know,' said Kate.

'Ask on,' replied Zoë blandly. 'I shan't promise that I won't tell you a lie.'

'Did he – did Giles leave you with child?'

Zoë threw back her head, revealing the length of her strongly-muscled throat; laughed, to show a mouthful of white, perfect teeth. 'You really must forgive my

rudeness,' she said when she had recovered her composure. 'Your sweetly archaic turn of phrase: "leave
you with child" – adorable! Next you will be asking
me if I begat. No, my dear Kate, your late husband and
my late lover did not leave me with child, nor did I
beget. Bad girls don't get themselves into trouble,
they're too smart. It's the good girls who get into
trouble.' She smirked and took another sip from her
glass.

'Then, if there was no child, why did he settle ten
thousand pounds a year on you?' demanded Kate.

Zoë lowered the glass. From her expression, Kate
could see that her question had struck home.

'My God!' said the other slowly. 'Someone's been
dishing the dirt to you all right, haven't they? How
much else do you know, I wonder?'

'Quite a lot,' said Kate. 'I know now why he settled
that money on you – now you've told me that there's no
child.'

Zoë drained her glass, set it down upon a small table,
reached up to the chimneypiece and took a cigarette
from out of a marquetry box. '*That* you do not know,
my dear,' she said firmly. 'That, my dear, was one
whopping great lie.'

'He gave you that money to buy you off,' said Kate.
'He was finished with you!'

Zoë's eyes flared. 'He did no such thing!' she hissed.
'I am not to be bought off, as you put it. No man
finishes with me. *I* call the tune. Always.'

'He went down to Plymouth that day,' said Kate,
'with the intention of breaking with you.'

'He did not!'

'He met you.'

'I wasn't there! I've never been near the place!'

'He told you it was all over between you. Offered the ten thousand a year. But – like you said just now – you aren't one to be bought off. It's you who tell the men in your life when to get out. But he was firm. So, in your anger – your insane rage – the rage of a woman spurned – you killed him!'

Zoë's eyes were wild and staring. 'You're mad!' she cried. 'I've always thought there was something crazy about you. You, with your buttoned-up, mealy-mouthed, virginal ways. He despised you, do you know that? He despised himself, too. Because of that brother of his. Though he despised you, he married you. For your looks, your talent. Yes, even for your title. He got a kick out of owning a real live Hon. I know all this. He spilled it out all over my pillow in the darkness, after we'd . . .'

'He loved me!' cried Kate. 'He loved me in the end. And that was why he went down and told you it was all over between you. And for that, you killed him!'

'*Prove it!*'

From out of her crocodile skin handbag, Kate took the envelope with the single word: *Darling* written in her dead husband's rakish italic; held it up for Zoë's regard.

'He left me a note,' she said simply.

The cigarette remained, unlit, between Zoë's fingers. After a few moments, she put it between her red-limned lips. The hand that reached out, took up a gas lighter, and applied it to the end of the cigarette was quite unwavering. Zoë was past all surprise.

'Well, my dear Kate,' she drawled. 'It almost looks as if you have me in something of a spot, haven't you?'

The woman's perfect composure – now that she had accepted the situation – was quite beyond belief. But then, as Kate recalled, Zoë had been an 'actress'. Actress, model, woman-about-town – one of the army of ubiquitous *demi-mondaines* who smile out from the pages of the glossies, caught in the company of the titled and the rich, mostly other women's husbands. Kate wondered how it squared with Church Gate Cottage, Wingham.

'I threw myself at him,' said Zoë blandly. 'Ooops! There I go – trotting out archaic little clichés. I believe the whole phrase is "threw myself at his head". Yes, I did that, all right. And he caught me. Am I boring you, dear?'

'Tell me,' whispered Kate. 'Tell me – everything.' (And when I have heard the worst, I shall be able to take the thing from out of my handbag, and . . .)

'Well, how cosy,' drawled Zoë. 'Are you sitting comfortably? Let's go.' She poured herself another generous measure of gin and added the remainder of the tonic. 'Where to begin? It started – as I think you may have been bright enough to guess – at your grotty party. I had had Peter Walker take me. The informative Peter. He was only too glad, for he already had the notion – quite correctly – that I was about ready to chuck him. You see, I had set my cap at Giles, having seen him

around. Ooops! There I go again. "Set my cap" –
more clichés.' She laughed tipsily. She really had had a
lot to drink.

'Please go on,' said Kate.

'Giles telephoned me the following day,' said Zoë.
'And was sharing my pillow within a week. How do
you like it so far?'

Kate closed her eyes. 'Go on.'

She heard the ice cubes tinkle in Zoë's glass as the
woman crossed the room and sat down on a sofa
opposite.

'Then came the Plymouth set-up. He would do his
work during the day and meet me in the evenings. We
spread a very wide net. Dined all over the West
Country. Stayed at a different hotel every time and
never registered together. As you must well know,
Giles was secretive to the point of extinction. Not
because it was really necessary; no way was anyone
going to report him back to you, and plenty knew. He
just liked the secrecy for its own sake.'

'Never let his right hand know what the left was
doing,' said Kate quietly, remembering the circumstances in which she had overheard her dead husband
being so described.

'My, we really are leaving no cliché unturned today,'
laughed Zoë. She took another draught from her glass.
'Want to hear any more?'

'I want to hear it all – every word!'

Zoë shrugged. 'You really are a devil for punish-
ment, kid. All right – so it was about then that I discovered his thing about his brother, and his king-sized

inferiority complex. Did I say he despised you? I
didn't get it quite right. It wasn't so much that he
despised you as that he found you to be a disappointment.'

Kate drew breath sharply. 'A – disappointment?'

'Like I said, you had the looks, the talent, the handle
to your name.' Head on one side, Zoë regarded the
other woman across the length of the room. 'He
thought he'd bought himself a glossy package that
would drive all the other boys wild with jealousy. But
you with your clinging, virginal ways, scared all the
other boys away. Giles, who'd taken you to give his
own inferiority a boost, found himself with a little
clinging vine that no one else would look at. That did
him no good at all. Hence – me.'

'Who are no clinging vine.'

'Right. In no time at all, Giles found I was cheating
him with another guy. He went wild. And his ego took
a jumbo boost when I promised to chuck the other
guy.'

'Which promise you did not keep, of course.'

'No way, baby. Zoë is all her own woman. No man
dictates to Zoë.'

'But then,' said Kate, 'in spite of the way you were
able to boost him, in the end he was the one to make
the break. Not you.'

Though the other woman's head was thrown into
shadow by the light from the window behind her, Kate
saw the danger sign of two vertical lines appear on her
brow.

Zoë said: 'I overplayed my hand. Your sort – the sort who've had it easy all your lives – have no conception what it's like to be my sort. There comes a time when you feel you're going crazy, when all you want is to know for certain who'll be sharing your pillow next year and paying the rent. I decided Giles would do for my permanent meal-ticket so I put it to him that he left you for me. That did it.'

'He knew then that he loved me.' Kate made no attempt to keep the joy, the pride, out of her voice.

'Don't kid yourself!' retorted Zoë harshly. 'He was happy enough with me while he knew that everything in trousers wanted me and that I was available to any good proposition. He didn't want me for a wife, or anything approaching a wife. No clinging vine – he already had one of those!'

'So he tried to buy you off,' said Kate. Her fingers trembled as she took hold of her crocodile skin hand-bag more tightly. 'Tell me what happened.'

Zoë rose and went over to the drinks table. Her step was unsteady. The chink of glass on glass; no longer was she pouring with deft expertise. The grating harshness remained in her voice as she resumed her story:

'It was an evening just like the rest,' she said. 'I went down to Plymouth by train as usual and Giles met me at the station – typically, he always parked in a side street where no one would see us. I checked into my hotel – the same hotel at which he was staying. We drove off to find a new place for dinner. On the way there, Giles stopped the Aston in a lay-by and said he

had something to tell me. I think I guessed right away
what he was going to say. His attitude to me was quite
different from what it had been before – before I put
my proposition to him. He was – shifty. I know the look
so well in men: when they've gone overboard, and
spent more money in a night club than they can afford
and hope to God that the management will take a
cheque and the cheque won't bounce so the little
woman back home won't find out. Giles was like that,
only he was shifty because he figured he had gone over
his head emotionally and wanted to pull out. He told
me as much; added that he had a farewell present for
me. And then I slapped the bastard across the mouth.'

'Go on,' said Kate.

'He didn't slap me back,' said Zoë. 'Always the
gentleman, Giles. He started up the car and drove. He
drove for an hour. Christ, why we didn't get picked up
I shall never know. He drove like a madman. I guess
he had some idea of cooling me down. No way. I got
madder by the moment. In the end, we came to this
place on the cliff, where he pulled up and turned to me.
"Darling Zoë," he said – I remember quite well he
called me "Darling Zoë" – "this is the end of the road
for you and me, so why not face up to it?" Then he put
his hand in his pocket and took out a long envelope.
"This is my parting gift, my dear," he told me. "No
one will ever know. It's been done very discreetly,
the way I always do things . . ." '

Zoë's voice trailed away.

'Go on!' cried Kate, rising.

'You wanna hear it?'

'Yes!'

Zoë rose also. Across the room, she was taller than Kate by half a head. She said: 'Something cracked in my head. There was a jack handle lying on the little back seat behind us. He always kept the inside of that car like a junk shop . . .'

'Yes, he did. He did,' said Kate. 'Go on!'

'It was so easy,' said Zoë. 'You wouldn't believe how easy. I didn't even hit him very hard. But the thing was very heavy. You could feel, through the handle, that it had really knocked him cold. Wanna hear the rest?'

'Go on!'

'I didn't panic. Strange how I didn't panic. All those years of night-clubbing with guys playing Russian roulette with their bank balances in the hope of sharing one's pillow hardens a girl in such circumstances, I guess. I picked up the long envelope lying on his lap. After all, I told myself, a few hundred pounds in dirty used notes won't come amiss . . .'

'Go on!'

'The hand-brake was on the dashboard, a kind of umbrella handle. I got out. Snicked off the hand-brake . . .'

'Go on!'

'I didn't even have to push. He'd stopped within feet of the edge and pointing right to sea. The Aston started to roll of its own accord. And then – you know what?'

'Go on!'

'He sort of recovered. Lifted his head from the steering-wheel. Gave a groan. I think he was looking about him as the front end went over the edge. He screamed on the way down. *What are you doing? What's that thing you've got in your hand?*'

The bodkin's point glittered evilly in the late sunlight of the summer's day that streamed through the window of Church Gate Cottage, the same sunlight that brightened Kate Hawksmoor's staring eyes as she advanced upon the other woman.

'I am going to kill you,' she said simply.

And then Zoë began to laugh: tipsy laughter with an edge of hysteria. She backed away from Kate, but only because she had lost her balance, not because she feared the threatening needle point. Catching the heel of her wooden-soled platform shoes in the edge of a rug, she fell backwards on to the sofa again, where she lay with her legs sprawled out before her, her hands pressed to her face, still in a paroxysm of mirthless laughter.

Put out of countenance, appalled to find herself with a murder weapon and a victim who would not play her role, Kate could only stand and stare.

'This is great!' cried Zoë. 'This is the greatest thing since wrapped bread. You really meant it, didn't you? Or did you?' Her eyes met Kate's – and they were narrowed in contempt. Totally uncaring. 'Well, if you did, why not go right ahead?' Her hand went to the neck of her shirt; tore it aside, buttons and all, baring her bronzed bosom. 'Have a go, darling. You'll only be anticipating the Grim Reaper by quite a little time.'

'What – what do you mean?' faltered Kate.

'I mean,' said Zoë, 'that you have come around too late to exact vengeance, my dear – save in a totally symbolic way.

'I'm already dying! Why else would Zoë Chalmers be holed up in a dump like *this*?'

CHAPTER XIII

ZOË HAD DOWNED yet another drink; yet somehow she seemed to have sobered up. She sat on the sofa, hands pressed between her knees, looking oddly wistful and little-girlish. Kate, who had cast aside the bodkin, watched her in mingled pity and horror.

It was leukæmia, and it was killing her. Zoë told this flatly and without emotion, just as she told how it had brought her to Church Gate Cottage, an odyssey that had begun on that Cornish clifftop three years previously, after she had murdered Giles.

'I left that clifftop just as fast as I could run,' she said. 'Luckily it was dark, so no one saw me. I stepped out of sight in the lanes every time I saw a car's headlights approaching. Then I came upon this transport café, with great juggernauts parked outside. I picked one with Dutch number plates and markings and laid in wait for the driver. He dropped me near my Plymouth hotel and I never let him get a look at my face.

'It's unbelievable, but two days passed before I got around to opening that envelope. And instead of finding a wad of used fivers, there was this deed, all signed, sealed and delivered, telling me that I had ten thousand a year for life. No one will ever know what that meant to me. It was like Aladdin's cave opening up. I was on my beam ends. I was never much of an actress, and I'd worn out my welcome on every casting couch in town.

As for the modelling game, I was suffering from a bad case of over-exposure, and I mean that literally; having posed nude a couple of times, I had put myself out of business as far as decently paid work was concerned.

'I went crazy. Bought myself a new wardrobe and gave my old one to Oxfam. Spent the summer in Ibiza and the winter in Kitzbühel. Little Zoë was the toast of wherever she went. It could have lasted for ever. Then – I began to feel not too well . . .' She buried her face in her hands.

'I think,' said Kate, 'that I will have a drink, after all.' She crossed to the table and poured herself a small gin. Zoë remained as she was for a long time, while Kate stood watching her, slowly revolving her glass between her fingers.

'Happily,' said Zoë at length, 'happily I went to a man who was willing not to mince matters after the diagnosis had been made, so I was left with all my options open. My inclination was to go on to the end playing Zoë the toast of town. But I couldn't keep it up. I get so damned tired so easily, and it shows in my looks. Hence, I have come to vegetate quietly in the country, where I flip over the pages of my snapshot albums, drink myself stupid, and wait for the end. Well – I don't think I could sit through the last reel, so I shall myself anticipate the end. I have the means to do so.' She looked up at Kate. 'So you see, my dear, I really meant it when I offered you the opportunity of doing the job for me. What are you going to do now?'

'I don't know,' said Kate.

'Tell the police?'

'What would be the point?'

'All you have to do is provide them with my name and the outline of the story. They could piece the rest of it together. I would stand trial and be found guilty. Then my end would be in a prison hospital. Dragging out my days, losing my looks with every passing day. And no means at hand to end it all. Yes, you would get your revenge in spades that way.'

Kate drained the glass and laid it quietly back upon the table. 'Thanks for the drink,' she said.

'You're going?'

'I've nothing to stay for.'

'You'll go to the police?' The other's eyes were upon her. It was a straight question with no strings attached. No entreaty.

'As I said before, what would be the point?'

Zoë watched her pick up the crocodile skin handbag and her scarf; made half a move to rise as Kate turned and walked to the open door. There was a crunch of footsteps on the path outside.

'That'll be Stan the fish man,' said Zoë.

Kate drew breath sharply when she saw them: two large figures in blue. There was a car with a winking blue light on its roof parked outside the gate, and another one was drawing up.

Zoë had come up behind her. She saw them. Cried out:

'*You lied to me, you bitch! You'd sent for them already!*'

'No! I didn't!'

The two policemen quickened their step when they saw and heard. Zoë backed away into the room, her eyes wide, shaking her head.

'I won't let them take me,' she whispered. 'Not that
– not to end up like that!'

She ran across the room, and through a door at the
far end, just as the police entered. One of them was
young and bearded. He had seen Zoë's departure.

'Which of you is Mrs Hawksmoor?' he demanded.

'I am,' said Kate.

'And that was Miss Chalmers?'

Kate nodded.

Zoë had locked the door behind her. They knocked,
rattled the handle.

'Open up, Miss Chalmers! This is the police!'

'You won't take her,' Kate heard herself saying. 'She
has the means – '

They had already begun to kick the door in when
there came the sound of a pistol shot from beyond.

The police were kindness itself, and drove Kate back to
London, where she was formally charged with the
theft of the Mini and remanded on bail, after which she
was escorted home by Detective Chief Superintendent
Alex Cushman himself, who sat beside the driver and
said nothing throughout, nor had he introduced himself to Kate; but he took a great interest in examining
her countenance in the rear-view mirror, a fact of which
she was uncomfortably aware. Cushman, it was, who
had arranged for her bail. He had his own reasons.

The Rolls-Royce was in its accustomed place outside the flat when they arrived. Cushman got out and
opened the car door for her; stood waiting while she

found her keys and admitted herself.

Home. She was home. Kate leaned back against the door and closed her eyes. The nightmare odyssey was over. One thing only remained to be resolved. The picture – *her* picture, the key to the enigma – was where she had left it. Finished, save for the face of the woman on the clifftop who was pushing the suitcase into the dark abyss. Kate took up her palette and brushes.The colours on the palette were still moist and workable, just as they had been when the knock upon the door had set in train a cycle of events that had led to Zoë Chalmers putting a pistol into her mouth.

She shuddered at the recollection, took a loaded brush and advanced towards the canvas . . .

I slept a little that night, and was calm again when I woke in the dawn. First, I cleaned up the mess of broken glass in the studio, then went up to the nursery, dragging with me a big suitcase from the box-room. A stiff measure of brandy buoyed me up for what had to be done, in spite of which I could not bring myself to open the curtains, but worked in semi-darkness that hid from me the worst details of what I had done the night before.

I put into the suitcase her favourite party dress, teddy-bear, the bracelet I had given her for her birthday: memento mori to go with her to oblivion. That was not too harrowing. I had to steel my nerve with another drink before I could go near the cot.

Pussy's limp, dead weight lay heavily in my arms, as, choked with horror, I lifted her out of the cot and laid her in the suitcase. One sightless blue eye stared up at me. Averting my

*gaze, I directed my trembling hand to cover the face with the
skirt of the dress.*

*A bloodless, white arm hung limply over the edge of the
case. It was curiously warm to the touch as I folded it gently
round the teddy-bear.*

'Goodbye, Pussy,' I whispered. And closed the lid . . .

It was over. The strange painting was finished. Kate
Hawksmoor laid aside her palette and brushed a stray
tendril of hair from her cheek; stood back to see the
effect, head on one side, lips pursed.

It was all there in the picture: the true account of her
love and motherhood. The history of betrayal, death,
and the renouncing of love.

The face of the woman on the clifftop was her face.

Sand martins were swooping and wheeling over the
cliffs at the wings of the beach. Two officers, the local
inspector and the station sergeant, plodded through the
deep sand towards the thin line of oily breakers that
curled sullenly along the edge of the bay. As far as the
horizon, the sea was like a sheet of beaten blue steel
across which crawled an eastward-bound coaster, its
haze of funnel smoke teased out like a streamer of grey
wool behind it. There was hardly a breath of air. The
two men were in shirtsleeves, and fanning their perspir-
ing faces with their caps.

Fifty yards from the low tide mark, they halted and
peered ahead, shielding their eyes against the early
glare. Presently, the inspector pointed to a small hump
that lay in the sand, deposited there by the retreating

tide. A pair of holidaymakers, out for an early morning bathe, had spotted it, and, guessing what it was, and being cosseted urbanites, and shrinking from the realities of mortal frailty, had not thought even to drag the pathetic piece of flotsam up above the tide line; but had simply phoned the police and reported that the dead body of a child had been washed up on 'their' beach.

The officers continued their advance. The going was firmer, now, on the hard, wet sand. Twenty yards from their goal, each instinctively slowed his step – such is the reluctance of even the hardiest soul to intrude upon mortal dissolution. Closer, still, each automatically pulled out his handkerchief and held it against his nostrils, as the sweet-sour stink of decaying seaweed and molluscs hinted at fouler miasmas yet to come.

The sergeant hung back, permitting his superior to make the first inspection of the remains. This the latter did – still with his handkerchief pressed against his nose and mouth – by kneeling in the sand and tentatively turning over the still form.

'Is it her, sir?' breathed the sergeant. 'Is it Pussy?' By now, everyone involved in the case was calling the missing child by her pet name, and it had also been taken up by the media.

The inspector did not answer; but gingerly lifted the skirt of the torn nightdress from the ravaged face. One blue eye hung out on a stalk of cotton. The head remained attached to the trunk by only a piece of string. Dirty white cotton-wool, swollen by immersion in the sea, protruded from rents in the skin.

'Good Gawd!' said the sergeant in a hushed whisper.
'It's nothing but a doll!'

'So much for Pussy,' said the inspector.

Cushman went alone to the orphanage in Kensington:
a handsome Edwardian mansion in a quiet street, with
a high wall built to protect its former millionaire
owner from the vulgar gaze of passers-by, and a garden
laid out in imitation of Balmoral, where the present
inmates, all in their blue-and-white check gingham
frocks, walked round and round the goldfish pond and
the rose arcade, hand in hand, from two to two-fifteen
every day.

Cushman was ushered into a bare, large room that
smelt of institutional antiseptic and floor polish. A tall
french window gave on to a conservatory. Beyond that,
through the Art Nouveau stained-glass windows, he
could see the little orphan girls taking their constitu-
tional, hand-in-hand, pair-by-pair, grave-faced, un-
speaking.

'Is it the Chief Superintendent?' Intent upon the
scene through the window, Cushman did not hear the
arrival of the Sister-in-charge. She came up behind
him, soft-footed in tennis shoes. Her bare arms were
mottled with liver-coloured blotches. She was a dumpy,
kind-looking woman in white, sleeveless overalls, a lace
coif, and the medal of some nursing order pinned to her
generous bosom.

'Sister Clancy.' Cushman took her extended hand in
his. 'It was good of you to respond so quickly.'

'I recognized the child immediately,' said the other.

'As soon as the picture came upon the screen, I said to the Bursar: "Mr Whittaker," I said, "that's our Polly, and that's a picture of dear sweet Mrs Hawksmoor!" And of course it was, for didn't they give her name over the loudspeaker just as I was saying it.'

'Polly?' said Cushman, and nodded thoughtfully.

'That's her name here,' said the matron. 'Indeed, that's the name upon her birth certificate, though Mrs Hawksmoor, it was, who gave her the pet name of Pussy. Seems as if she had a little girl of her own of that name. You see her out there, Chief Superintendent? The one coming round now. With the fair hair.'

'I see her,' said Cushman.

She came towards them, turning at the end of the rose arcade, skirting the side of the conservatory; grave-faced like the rest, hand-in-hand with her companion.

Cushman saw her as the child in the painting that Kate Hawksmoor had made of her: sad-eyed, with blonde plaits, head bowed, shoulders sagging; a child bearing a weight of sorrows too heavy for the slender sum of her years.

'Poor mite,' said Sister Clancy. 'The father disappeared at her birth, and the mother treated her the way that bad children use animals. She came to us a battered baby. I doubt if she'll ever be right enough to take her place in the world.'

Cushman cleared his throat. 'Um – is she, is Polly, in any way afflicted, Sister? Physically, I mean. Or mentally.'

'There's epilepsy there,' replied Sister Clancy.

'Epilepsy – ah,' said Cushman, nodding. 'Yes, that

would about fit the bill.'

'What was that you said, Chief Superintendent?' asked the other.

Cushman was fumbling for his pipe. 'Do you mind if I smoke, Sister?' he asked.

The woman beamed, folded her arms, regarded him fondly. 'It's a man's privilege, I always say,' she declared.

Packing tobacco into the bowl, Cushman glanced sidelong at the crocodile of little girls who continued to file past. The child with the blonde plaits went by again; her expression, her whole demeanour, unchanged.

'How did Mrs Hawksmoor come in contact with you, Sister?' he asked. 'And with Pussy – I mean Polly.'

'Why, it was through Lady Coxborough,' replied the other. She gave a sniff of disapproval. 'Not that I've any time for that lot of idle biddies. But Mrs Hawksmoor, she's different from the rest.'

'And she became a sort of fairy godmother to Pussy – took her out for treats, that sort of thing?'

'Every Sunday afternoon without fail,' said Sister Clancy. 'Mostly it would be the Zoo, sometimes a trip on the river in a water bus to Kew or to Greenwich. And lately, Mrs Hawksmoor, she's been writing the Governors to ask if she can take Polly away for holidays to her cottage in Kent, maybe with a view to adopting the child.' The woman paused. 'Chief Superintendent, tell me now, is Mrs H. in some kind of bad trouble?'

Cushman disregarded the question. He said: 'What are the Governors' views on Mrs Hawksmoor adopting the child, Sister? What are *your* views?'

The woman raised an eyebrow, gave Cushman the
shrewd glance of a person who is making a quick appraisal of another's capacity for sympathetic compre-
hension. Then she said: 'Well, the Governors are un-
decided, and that's a fact. You see, Chief Superintendent, the child's a difficult one, and it isn't only the
epilepsy – that wouldn't normally be a bar to allowing
her to go out to adoption. When a child as young as she
was has suffered what she did, there's more damage
done than can be cured by a few kind words and good
intentions. Mrs Hawksmoor has learned that already,
though, God bless her, she's never once turned against
Polly.'

Cushman nodded. 'And that squares with your views,
Sister? You wouldn't be happy about Mrs Hawksmoor adopting the child?'

Sister Clancy thought for a few moments and said:
'You see, it's like this. All else aside, we're realists here.
We're trained to look after the likes of that poor mite,
while Mrs Hawksmoor, she's nothing to rely on but her
lovely instincts. And she's a fine woman. But, Chief
Superintendent, she's a woman who's already had a lot
of sorrow in her life. It shows in her eyes, don't you
think? I wouldn't want to be party to encouraging her
to bring in more sorrow. That's why I wouldn't be
happy – not yet, at any rate, not till she and Polly have
grown closer – for her to adopt the child. Do you see
what I mean?'

'I do,' said Cushman.

A handbell rang out in the garden, borne by a pretty

girl in mauve nurse's uniform. At the sound, the children broke files and flocked about her, their faces alight with sudden pleasure, reaching out to take her hands, the skirt of her apron. One child only hung back: the child Polly. She watched from afar, eyes sullen and suspicious, mouth turned down, fingers twined together in tortuous convulsions.

Sister Clancy sighed. 'Well, will you look at that! And another time, she'll be the first to run to Nurse Delaney and throw her arms about her.'

'I'll be going, Sister,' said Cushman. 'Thank you for all your help.'

'Well, I've been of little help and that's for sure,' said Sister Clancy. 'And you never did answer my question – and isn't that just like a policeman? Is Mrs Hawksmoor in trouble?'

'I think she has been in very bad trouble,' replied Cushman, tapping the upturned bowl of his pipe against the palm of his hand. 'But whether she's free of it now, I don't yet know.'

CHAPTER XIV

THE PRESS, drawn by conflicting rumours about a missing child and the possibility of an imminent arrest for murder, had by then laid siege to Kate Hawksmoor's studio flat, thereby greatly lowering the tone of the immediate neighbourhood and constraining more than one tenant to make formal complaint to the police. The police continued to maintain a nominal watch upon the premises, but the solitary uniformed constable on the gate at the end of the drive had been given no authority to obstruct the passage of such reporters as chanced their luck by knocking on the door to gain admission – and they were many.

Cushman had bidden Orville to announce his arrival by posting a note to that effect through Kate Hawksmoor's letter-box, and she, who had not been answering the door nor the constantly jangling telephone, having read it, was quick to open up and admit him when he arrived punctually at three o'clock, having come more or less straight from the orphanage.

Three importuning reporters made to enter with Cushman; he thrust them back.

'I hate those men,' said Kate. 'It's like having human vultures hovering over one's every move. I've only to peer through the curtains and they wave up at me, and someone rings me from the call-box at the end of the street immediately afterwards.'

'It's not a gentleman's job,' said Cushman. 'How could it be so, Mrs Hawksmoor? Selling vacuum-cleaners from door to door isn't in it. They have to be hard and nasty to survive. Say, a little lad's been found murdered. You've been sent to put your foot in the door and get a snapshot of the kiddie from the parents. The father's driving a truck somewhere up north and the mother's going mad. Your editor's holding the presses for that picture. There's a framed photo of the murdered kid on the mantelpiece – ' he shrugged – 'who's to call it stealing if you slip it under your coat?'

Kate looked at him: a man of middle years, about forty-five, with a red face, clipped moustache, curiously kindly grey eyes that met one's own and held them – but not with aggression. A stocky, strong body, running to a paunch: an athlete past his best – her artist's eye, trained in life class and cast room, assessed and docketed his physique faultlessly. Her intuition got to work upon his character. The eyes were the only clue she had; the rest was all policeman.

Cushman regarded Kate. She looked remarkably better than she had looked when he assisted her delivery back home the previous evening; was dressed in well-cut jeans, a suede jacket over a T-shirt. She really is a beautiful creature, he thought. And that Sister Clancy was right: there's a sorrow in her eyes – not that it detracts from the tremendous effect.

'Would you care for some tea?' murmured Kate.

'I don't want to bother you.'

'No bother. It's all ready. I was expecting you. You were on time. All I have to do is boil up the kettle again. Please make yourself comfortable.'

He watched her walk out of the studio room: grace-
ful as a Greek statue come to life, with a total physical
unselfconsciousness.

In her kitchen, Kate bowed her head over the
muttering kettle and closed her eyes. Oh God, give me
the strength to go through with it. The part about Zoë
Chalmers, which I suppose is his immediate concern –
I shall be able to cope with well enough. But the rest –
if he knows, or guesses, about Pussy. How shall I be
able to sit and talk about it rationally without breaking
down and betraying myself? Give me strength! Oh
please, give me strength!

'It's China tea,' she said coolly, wheeling the trolley
into the studio room. 'I hope you don't mind, but it's
all I have at the moment, for I'm almost completely out
of provisions, and even the milk is the dried variety.
For some reason, the milkman's stopped calling. Do
you suppose he thinks he won't be paid?'

'To tell you the truth,' said Cushman, 'I can't tell
one from t'other. It's all tea to me. What nice cups and
saucers.'

'Rockingham.'

'And very fine examples of Rockingham, too.'

'You are interested in china, Chief Superintendent
Cushman?'

'It is my hobby, Mrs Hawksmoor. My speciality is
Meissen.'

'Oh, that's interesting,' said Kate. 'I have a . . .'

'Shepherdess. Yes, I've seen and admired it.'

Of course he had. She had almost forgotten that this man, this guest who had dropped in for tea, had had the free run of her home while she had been away. The signs of his passing had greeted her upon her return. Not that he, and presumably his many minions, had made any mess; but crockery had been used, washed up, and put back differently. And over all had hung – still faintly hung – the smell of tobacco, which she never used. She wondered how far he had pried into her private affairs, and felt relieved that she had never in her life kept a diary, nor saved old letters.

But there was the picture, the painting of the oval-shaped room, now finished. She stole a glance to where it stood upon the easel, draped in a cloth. And was uncomfortably aware that he had observed the glance.

'Milk?' she murmured. 'Of course, it's only dried.'

'Yes, please.'

'Biscuit? They, also, are rather dry.' She smiled nervously at her own whimsy.

'Thank you, no.' Cushman took a sip of his tea, regarding Kate over the rim of the cup. He was not deceived by her veneer of calm; here, he told himself, was a frightened woman, a woman ridden with guilt. But of *what* was she guilty? Time to find out.

'The inquest is set for Thursday,' he said.

'Inquest?' And she drew breath sharply.

'On Miss Chalmers. You will be summoned to attend.'

'I see. Yes, of course.'

'The verdict will be suicide, naturally. A mere

formality. What was your reason for stealing a car and driving all that way to see the woman, Mrs Hawksmoor?'

'I – I think I went to kill her,' said Kate.

'Because of your husband.'

'You know about that?'

Cushman said: 'We learned that he had settled a very considerable annuity on her a few days before his death. Armed with that information, we had a search made of every hotel register in a twenty-mile radius of Plymouth Hoe. And found what we were after. In almost every case, the Chalmers woman had registered her home address as Church Gate Cottage, Wingham, which was her weekend retreat at that time. Do I take it that our fellows arrived just in time to prevent you from carrying out your intent, Mrs Hawksmoor?'

Kate shook her head. 'No. I was just about to leave. What there was between us was already settled. Finished.'

'Mmm.' Cushman drained his cup and set it down. 'So you've been at work again already, Mrs Hawksmoor. At your painting, I mean.'

Kate's cup and saucer fell from her fingers and shattered themselves upon the parquet floor. In the silence that hung in the air afterwards, she stared at him uncomprehendingly.

'I can smell the fresh paint,' he explained.

'Of course,' she whispered.

'Care to show it to me?'

She did not reply, but rose and walked across the wide sweep of floor to where the easel stood, and the draped picture. Without turning to face Cushman, she pulled aside the covering and stood with it hanging from her fingers. Cushman came up behind her.

'So it *was* you,' he said.

'Who else?'

'But the thing in the suitcase was only a doll.'

'Yes. Only a doll.'

'But where is the real Pussy? Where is your daughter, Mrs Hawksmoor? Did she ever exist?'

'Pussy existed,' said Kate Hawksmoor. 'She lived and breathed, and was entirely beautiful and all I ever wished for to fill the aching void left by my husband's death.

'And I killed her.'

'I have lived on the edge of madness,' said Kate Hawksmoor calmly. 'And now I am sane. The process has taken three years, during which time, I escaped from hurt by retreating into a world of imagery that existed only in my own head.'

Cushman marvelled at her composure. Having been brought to it, the fear and the guilt seemed to have been shed from her; she appeared willing, even eager, to tell him everything.

'It began,' said Cushman, 'with the birth of your daughter, I take it?'

'I suppose to every woman,' said Kate, 'the birth of a first child is a once and only experience. And how much more so it was for me, because the new life I held in my arms was the only thing I had left of Giles.'

'Then the child was not stillborn?' said Cushman.

'My first thought was that it might have been born dead.'

Kate closed her eyes, pressed the palms of her hands together.

'Pussy lived,' she whispered. 'The old doctor attended us the morning after and pronounced her to be perfect. Perfect – what an understatement! She was rapture. I could not bear her to be out of sight for a moment, but lay watching her asleep in her cot by the side of my bed. Nannie scolded me because I was forever picking her up at the slightest pretext; she would take her from me and put her down again; but as soon as the old dear's back was turned, I would reach out for her . . .' Her voice trailed away.

'Take your time, Mrs Hawksmoor,' said Cushman gently. 'And anything that hurts you too much – just miss out.'

'I have to say it out loud,' said Kate. 'Once and for all, I have to face reality. I killed my child, Chief Superintendent. I killed her with the rapture of over-loving. I took her in my arms and held her close. I fell asleep. While I slept, my baby suffocated, slipping from sleep into death.'

The clock on the studio chimneypiece tinkled the hour. Cushman shifted in his seat; it sounded an intolerable intrusion upon the silence.

Presently, Kate continued: 'Mercifully, I have no recollection of the moment of realization, because the shock drove me out of my mind. Nor did Nannie ever intrude into my madness, but, hoping and praying that it would pass, played my game of make-believe.

Pretended that Pussy was still alive, that the un-
speakable had not happened.

'I think it's possible that she let me continue to nurse
my dead baby for some while. I remember waking up
in the night to find that she was no longer in my arms.
I remember wandering round the cottage, calling for
her by name. I remember Nannie persuading me that
she was safe and well, soothing me and putting me back
to bed. Laying something in my arms.'

'Laying – what?' interjected Cushman, leaning
forward in his seat.

'It was a doll from my husband's old toy cupboard,'
said Kate. 'They used to tease him when he was a little
boy because he liked to play with dolls. On a desperate
impulse, Nannie gave me the doll – something connected with my husband – and I accepted it.

'From that day I lived out my life in fantasy, with
Nannie Porter acting as handmaiden to my fantasy.
And, later, her sister also: the two dear old biddies
eating their hearts out, I don't doubt, and praying for
my recovery.

'I recovered – slowly. But still my mind wouldn't
accept the fact of my child being dead. It would have
made the break too complete, you see: the break with
my dead husband. Nannie came with me when I
registered the live birth. How she kept that old doctor
at bay, I shall never know. I expect she telephoned
him that we were returning to London. Nothing
happened to disturb my fantasy. And when we did
return to London, the doll came with us, cradled in
Nannie's arms in the back of the Rolls. That night, it

lay in a fairy-tale cot that I had had made.

'Two years went by before half of my mind began to accept the fact of my self-deception, but it made no difference; the fantasy persisted. It was my only comfort. That, and my painting. In the summer of the second year, I went to a private view of work done by a girl who had been a fellow student at the Royal College. She made most marvellous life-sized dolls as art objects. People bought them to sit around the house, they had quite a vogue. As soon as I walked into that gallery, I saw – Pussy.

'She was just as I'd always imagined her. The image of her father. His child to perfection, with soft skin and eyes that looked real enough to weep. I bought her. Discarded the baby doll. She became – Pussy.'

'At about this time,' said Cushman, 'you began to take up your work again with Lady Coxborough. Have I got it right?'

'It was part of the healing process,' said Kate. 'As I grew clearer in my mind, I had the urge to widen my horizon. I volunteered to work with children. There was this little girl at the orphanage – her name's Polly.'

'And she became, in a sense, Pussy?'

'In a sense,' said Kate. 'The rational half of my mind, that part which was healing, began to be drawn towards the living child, so that the doll and the real person became inextricably mixed up in my thoughts. When Polly and I were together, she became, in a very real sense, the little girl that my dead baby would have grown into. And the doll – just a doll.'

'The Brierleys,' said Cushman. 'Now, Colin Brierley – who, by the way, was arrested for fraud at London airport yesterday – had never before thought to mention, nor had his wife, that they had only ever seen your child the once. That was in this flat a year ago.'

Kate nodded. 'It was a wet Sunday,' she said. 'Polly came to tea and the Brierleys arrived uninvited. She came to borrow money. There was no question of a deliberate deception on my part. They accepted the child as mine unquestioningly. I'm sorry Colin's in trouble, but I've never liked him.'

'Then there's Mrs Holdheim,' said Cushman. 'She who you used to employ as a daily cleaner. We only traced her late last evening. She could have told us straight away that there was no child. Only a life-sized doll.'

'Poor Mrs H.,' said Kate. 'She must have thought me very odd.'

'She spent three years in a Nazi concentration camp,' said Cushman. 'With that experience, she not only finds nothing odd any longer, but keeps her opinions to herself. Add to that, you're an artist, and in Mrs Holdheim's book that excuses all sorts of odd behaviour. By the way, Mrs Hawksmoor, while I was here, I naturally looked around quite a lot.'

'Of course,' said Kate flatly.

'I saw your pictures. The ones stacked up in the storeroom.'

'The Mother and Child sequence,' said Kate. 'Yes, I worked on them right through the period when I was clawing my way back to sanity. They saved me. – They and the doll fantasy.'

'I was a bit puzzled, Mrs Hawksmoor, and I don't deny it,' said Cushman, 'to find that someone – presumably yourself – had destroyed one of the pictures by slashing it from end to end.'

'It happened the night when I was shocked back into sanity at last,' said Kate. 'The night when I learned that the man I had mourned for three years, whose child I had borne and lost, had been faithless to me. I had a lot to drink, and I am not used to drink. I spent all my fury and frustration on that picture – it wasn't very good. I had never really liked that particular canvas, and I'm a great one for destroying bad work.'

'Then you destroyed Pussy,' said Cushman.

'I destroyed a doll,' said Kate flatly. 'A poor thing of tat and stuffing upon which I had squandered all those long, empty days and nights of hungry love. Still half-drunk, yet sane in mind, I drove down to Cornwall and made an end to my fantasy by throwing one unrequited love after the other. Then I came back home and painted the picture you see here, which traces the steps that took me to that clifftop.' She spread her hands. 'And now I am set free. I can live with my grief, with my regrets. I can begin to cobble together the broken ends of my existence. As someone once said: today is the first day of the rest of my life.'

Cushman nodded. 'You'll do it, Mrs Hawksmoor,' he said. 'You'll do it real fine.'

Orville was waiting for him outside, having arrived in a patrol car whose radio was still squawking.

'Anything from Goudley?' demanded Cushman.

'They've had half the garden up,' said Orville. 'And they found the remains of a newborn infant buried under a tulip tree. What'll the charge be, sir? Is it infanticide, or concealing a stillbirth?'

'It was an accident,' said Cushman. 'The mother overlaid the baby only a few hours after birth and went half out of her mind in consequence. It was the old nurse who buried the baby, and she's beyond our reach now. There'll be an inquest. The coroner will hear Mrs Hawksmoor's evidence and she will convince him as she's convinced me. It will be Accidental Death, and deepest sympathy – well-deserved sympathy, I may add – will be expressed for the bereaved mother. And I've a notion that Mrs Hawksmoor will summon up the fortitude to grace the proper funeral of her dead child with courage and dignity.'

Orville's long, clever face turned to regard his chief. 'She seems to have made a very strong and favourable impression on you, sir,' he said.

Cushman pulled out his pipe, a move that won him a wrinkle of distaste from his subordinate's sensitive nostrils. 'I'll tell you about Mrs Hawksmoor, Mark,' he said. 'I've been a plain man all my life. Aside from being a copper, my only interests lie in my garden and my modest collection of china. Leaving the garden aside, you could say that, by learning to appreciate Meissen, I've extended my horizon – the horizon of a plain man – by a hundredfold. That's to say I've come to appreciate that there's a world that I can dimly reach out and touch the edge of. Mrs Hawksmoor,

Mark, inhabits that world, walks in it and is part of it the way I live and walk in the world of the plain man.'

'An artist,' said Orville. 'I take your point. She's an artist.'

Cushman beamed at his subordinate like a man who unexpectedly finds that he is the owner of a talking horse; pointed his pipe at him. 'That's right, Mark, you've got it in one. Mrs Hawksmoor's an artist, which is to say she's not to be judged by the yardstick of the plain man. Or the plain woman. Now, a plain woman, if she accidentally kills her newborn babe, she either gets over it and has another one right quick – or she goes mad with grief. And if she goes mad, she stays mad. There's no way back for her, not for the plain woman. By killing her kid, she's violated the few and simple rules of her sort, and can never look at herself again.'

'But the artist's different, that's your argument?' said Orville. 'There's a way back for the artist.'

Cushman stabbed him approvingly in the chest with the stem of his pipe. 'You get brighter by the hour, lad. You've got it in one again. The artist has a way back. Forget about the doll. That was a prop, to see her through the worst of it. The way back for her was that series of pictures you admired so much.'

'They're great,' said Orville. 'I'm no judge, but I know what I like. They say everything there is to say about Motherhood. But – hey, sir! She destroyed one of them. Ripped it from top to bottom and back again. Where's your artist there? Where's your creativity?'

'I'm glad you asked that,' replied Cushman. 'That

brings me to my final point. I quizzed Mrs Hawksmoor
on that one, 'cos I was as puzzled as you. She answered
me without turning a hair. Admitted that she was
drunk when she did it (as she was drunk when she
ripped up the doll, but she did that for a quite different
reason), and that she was venting her fury at her husband for cheating on her. But she had no regrets for the
ruined picture. It wasn't up to her standard, you see,
Mark. It was a failure. So she cut it to ribbons. Quite
calculatingly.'

'Hard,' said Orville. 'You're implying that she's
hard inside.'

Cushman's pleasure at his subordinate's prescience
was now quite complete. 'You took the very words
right out of my mouth, Mark,' he declared. 'That's it.
They're hard inside, artists. They suffer more than the
plain man, but they've got this hardness, this gem-like
flame inside, that keeps 'em going. Once that's ex-
tinguished, they're destroyed as artists and as people;
but while it's still alight, or even only flickering, they
just beaver on. And that's why I say that Mrs Hawksmoor will win through. I've no doubts about her. Not
now.'

He got out of Orville's patrol car. The newspaper-
men were still hovering. They had been watching the
exchange between the two detectives. One of them
made to come forward and put a question, or maybe
a host of questions.

'What about these cowboys?' said Orville.

'Give 'em nothing,' said Cushman. 'They'll have the

two inquests. Let 'em make of that what they will. And there'll be Mrs Hawksmoor's appearance for nicking the car.'

'She'll get a suspended sentence for that?'

'For sure. See you, Mark. You know, I think it's going to be a fine evening. Time to mow my lawn and do a few odd jobs in the greenhouse. See you tomorrow.'

'See you, sir.'

Orville gazed for a brief moment at his chief's stocky form and then got out of the patrol car to address himself to the newspaper reporter, who was already upon him, smiling false familiarity, nicotine-stained fingers fumbling a proffered packet of fags, lips already framing a question.

CHAPTER XV

ALL THE ENDS were drawn together. The history of
Giles, of Pussy, of a love reaching beyond death and
dissolution. Kate slumped on the floor of her studio,
leaned back against the wall, and examined anew the
sequence of 'Motherhood' that she would surely send
to Mr Grosse early in the coming week. She had rooted
around in her pantry and found a half-consumed
packet of her favourite breakfast cereal, which tasted
not half bad, even with reconstituted, powdered milk.
A beaker of unsweetened coffee completed this, her
first and only meal of the day. The reporters, blessedly,
had drifted away, some of them pausing only to drop
notes through the letter-box, none of which she had
bothered to open before consigning to the kitchen
disposal unit. Tomorrow, she must go shopping.

Decidedly, there was nothing to add to the Motherhood sequence. Nothing to add or subtract. A certain
sweetness of colour in the later canvases was, surely,
more than offset by the uncompromising severity of the
drawing. Perhaps put a glaze over one or two passages
where one's exuberance had promoted a little too
much of that lush greenery, that bravura of brush-
work . . .

The phone rang. She never took her eye from the
nearest canvas as she picked up the receiver.

'Is that you, Kate?' It was Jock Carter.

'Hello,' she said. 'Hello, Jock.'

'Are you all right?'

'Yes, I'm fine.'

'Well. Mmm. The *Polizei* were a trifle, you know, pushy, when they picked me up for driving the Rolls. Nothing to worry about, I hope?'

'Not now, Jock,' she said.

'Well, I thought,' he said, 'since the cheque will be cleared by Tuesday, which is the day after tomorrow, and that means I'll own the Rolls on Tuesday . . . well, to put it short, why don't we mark the occasion by having dinner together on Tuesday? What do you say, Kate?'

A butterfly made its fluttering, uncertain way through her window. Kate assisted its flight by moving aside, blowing gently towards it, to prevent the gorgeous creature from colliding with a potted tobacco plant. Pussy, my darling one – and you, my Giles, my dearest love – I shall never forget you. Blessedly, for all the mistakes of our lives, for all the stupidity and the follies, there are such tremendous consolations.

'You see, Kate, I've a notion to take the Rolls to the Continent. Right away. Head south for the sun while the summer lasts. How does that grab you, Kate? Are you hearing me?'

'I can't come to dinner on Tuesday, Jock,' she said. 'I'm very sorry.'

'Hell, that's a pity, Kate.'

'But ring me, I beg you, when you come back from your journey to the sun. And tell me all about it. I shall look forward to that.'